On Fallen Wings

JULIE NELSON

◆DOUBLE INFINITY BOOKS◆

On Fallen Wings

First published by Double Infinity Books 2025

First edition ISBN: 979-8-9992290-0-7

To the ones who hold on,
long after letting go seemed easier.

Content Warning

This book contains scenes of fantasy violence, magical coercion, captivity, emotional manipulation, blood, and hallucinatory sequences that may be unsettling to some readers.

Kingdom of Constalatia

Drowned Vale

Court of Embers

Moth Cliffs

Starcliff Falls

Human Realm

Laurelglade

Aqueduct

Bellwater

Ruins

Corvan's home

Blackfen

Pronunciation Guide

Constalatia – Con-sta-lay-she-ya
Nisrine – Nis-reen
Corvan – Core-van
Lonan – Loh-nan
Olesia – Oh-lee-sha
Cherith – Chair-ith
Seren – Seh-ren
Elaila – E-lay-la
Dade – Day-d
Eidolon – I-dole-en

Chapter 1

In the heart of an ancient forest, where the trees whispered secrets older than the stars themselves, Princess Nisrine stood at the edge of a glimmering pond. Its silver waters shimmered, reflecting the light of tiny, twinkling fireflies that circled the clearing like stars fallen to the earth. She lifted a delicate hand, fingers brushing the cool surface, and the water rippled in response to her touch.

Tall and striking, Nisrine possessed an otherworldly grace. Her long, dark auburn hair cascaded down her back in waves, catching the faint glow of the fireflies as if woven with strands of twilight itself. Her large hazel eyes, framed by thick lashes, held depths of curiosity and longing. Her pointed Fae ears, a mark of her heritage, peeked through the silken tresses, listening to the wind's whispered truths.

Her wings, translucent and iridescent, caught the moonlight, casting soft, colorful shadows across the moss-covered stones. They were the mark of her lineage, with the faintest hint of lavender and jade. Beautiful, yes, but also a symbol of her burden. Her wings were as fragile as her kingdom's peace. The kingdom of Constalatia.

Nisrine's realm was a world of delicate balance, where ancient magic flowed like a living current through the soil, the air, and even the very light itself. The Fae's magical power was not just in their wings or the spells they cast, but lived in the subtle weaving of unseen energy, threads of raw force that intertwined with nature's pulse. They could send magic outward in silence, or speak words in the ancient Fae tongue to deepen its strength. But the magic demanded harmony; every act, every choice rippled outward. Yet, with each flutter of her wings, she felt the weight of responsibility press down on her, the pressure of expectations from her elders, her court, and most of all, the realm itself.

Her father, King Lonan, had always warned her of the dangers that lurked beyond their realm. He used fear as a weapon to keep the balance in check. But Nisrine was not like her father. She had always longed for the unknown. The distant hum of the human world, their strange ways, and the stories they whispered of magic beyond the realm's borders. She couldn't resist it.

Nisrine lay on her stomach with her head resting lightly on her arm, watching the ripples continue in the pond. The pond was a special place that she shared with her mother, but ever since her disappearance, this place no longer brought Nisrine the same comfort it used to. It was once a place of happiness, but now, no amount of serenity could ease the dull ache that settled in Nisrine's chest.

Queen Cherith had been the heart of the realm, the bridge between the old ways and the dreams of a future that no one else dared to believe in. She had spoken of a time when Fae and humans lived in harmony, when magic was not feared but revered. She had taught Nisrine the ways of their people, had nurtured the strength within her, had watched with knowing eyes as Nisrine's magic grew more powerful than she herself understood.

And she had told stories.

Nisrine's favorite memory was one summer evening beneath the silver boughs of the Moonwillow tree. Cherith had braided daisies into Nisrine's hair as the twilight deepened, her voice soft and warm as she told tales of the human world.

"Did you know they once believed the stars were pinholes in the fabric of the sky?" Cherith had asked with a smile, her fingers deftly weaving through the strands. "And that if you stood still long enough, you could hear your soul whisper through the trees?"

Nisrine giggled. "That's not real."

"No," Cherith said gently. "But it's beautiful. Humans imagine things into truth, and sometimes that magic is stronger than ours. It's different. Wild. But it speaks to something old in all of us."

That night, Nisrine had looked up at the sky with new eyes, wondering if somewhere beyond the veil, someone was dreaming of her too.

And then, one day, Cherith was gone. Vanished without a trace. No warning, no final words. Just whispers of shadowed corridors and unanswered questions. Some claimed she had been taken. Others believed she had left of her own will, crossing into the human world in search of something lost.

Nisrine was just as lost as the others. All she knew was that her mother would not have abandoned her. She would not have left her father to rule alone.

And yet, she had.

Nisrine wanted to ask her what she should do now. If she should listen to her father's warnings or follow the pull in her heart, the same pull her mother once spoke of. But no answer would come.

Reluctantly, she sat up, brushing the dirt from her palms. The forest behind her was quiet, the sacred silence offering no comfort. She had come here for answers. The trees had none.

It was time to go back.

She glanced toward the outline of the castle, distant but looming. Her heart clinched. The last time she'd stood in the throne room, her voice had cracked as she pleaded: "Just send a scout. One. She could still be alive!"

Her father hadn't even looked at her. He'd kept his gaze fixed on the window, where the forest stretched endlessly beyond the glass. His reply had been cool, measured, as if he were closing a ledger rather than speaking of his vanished wife and queen.

"Cherith made her choice. And we do not chase ghosts."

That had shattered something. Not just hope, but the image of who he once was. Of who she once thought him to be. But today, something in her refused to let it end there. Maybe she was clinging to scraps. Maybe she was foolish. But she would try again.

She rose to her feet. Her wings stirred behind her, slow and shimmering. She pushed off the earth, lifting into the air, and glided toward the castle. The cool night air brushed against her skin, but beneath it, she felt something else. A pull. Subtle, almost imperceptible, like an invisible thread tugging at her, calling her back toward the depths of the forest.

She hesitated midair, her brows knitting together.

And then, she dismissed it.

Turning her gaze forward, she pressed on toward home. She took in the sight of the Kingdom of Constalatia. The castle rose like a vision from a dream, its iridescent stones shimmering under the moonlight. Waterfalls cascaded in the distance, feeding into the endless forests that stretched beyond the jagged peaks of the mountains. Vines of silver and sapphire wove up the high towers, and crystalline flowers bloomed with an otherworldly glow.

Inside, the grand hall was alive with revelry. King Lonan sat among his court, surrounded by guards and nobles, their laughter and songs echoing through the chamber as ale flowed freely. His voice rose above the noise, measured, regal, tinged with the kind of gravitas he reserved only for recounting his victories. Any hope Nisrine had for a meaningful conversation with her father faded.

On Fallen Wings

She stepped back from the threshold, the warmth and noise of the room spilling out around her like smoke, stifling and sharp. The doors closed with a dull thud, sealing it off.

Seren was waiting at the end of the corridor, leaning against a column in the flickering torchlight. His arms were crossed, but when he saw her face, he stood straighter. He was one of the Royal Guard, sworn protector of the Fae, and her oldest friend. His violet wings, darker than her own, shimmered faintly at the edges with threads of gold.

"No luck?" he asked, his voice quiet. He didn't need her to answer, his gaze had already softened, like he had hoped, but not expected, a different answer.

She shook her head, her voice low. "No. He's too deep in his own legend. Talking about victories he hasn't won. There's no space in him for listening."

Seren exhaled, looking down the hallway as though he could see through stone. "There hasn't been for a long time."

They stood in silence for a moment, the distant noise of revelry echoing through the stone like something haunting instead of joyous.

Seren glanced down the corridor again, then back at her. "You'll try again?"

"I have to." Nisrine's voice was quiet but certain.

Seren gave a slow nod. "Then I'll walk you to your room."

She smiled faintly. "Still guarding me after all this time?"

"Always," he said simply.

They walked in silence, the flicker of the torchlight casting long shadows along the walls. At her door, Seren paused, glancing at her with something unreadable in his expression.

"Goodnight, Nis."

"Goodnight," she replied. "And thank you."

He didn't answer, just dipped his head in a slight bow and waited until the door shut behind her before stepping away.

Chapter 2

The morning sun poured through the stained-glass windows, casting jeweled colors across the long breakfast table. A dozen kinds of bread steamed on silver platters: honeyed rye, citrus brioche, seed-studded flatbreads. Bowls of berries glistened with frost. There were poached pheasant eggs covered with dill garnish, carved fruit arranged in spirals, and thin slices of venison smoked over alderwood. It was all too perfect. Too staged.

Nisrine sat stiffly at the table, her plate barely touched.

King Lonan arrived at last, robed in slate-gray velvet, his silver hair combed back. He didn't greet her. He never did, not formally. Just a glance, and then he began slicing into his eggs.

Julie Nelson

She waited until the room had settled, until the clank of plates dulled into a hum.

"I want to speak of her," she said, voice low but firm. "Of mother."

Lonan didn't look up. "You already know my answer."

"I don't," Nisrine said calmly. "Because every time I ask, you say nothing or turn away. That's not an answer."

His knife scraped across his plate. "What more is there to say?"

"I don't believe she left us by choice," Nisrine continued, keeping her voice steady. "And neither do others."

Lonan finally met her gaze. His expression was carved stone, cold and unimpressed. "Others believe many things. That doesn't make them true."

"She wouldn't have just disappeared," Nisrine said. "Not without a word. Not without me."

Lonan set down his utensils with a click. "I've let you mourn her. I've let you ask your questions. But you forget your place."

"My place is beside the truth," she said.

He gave a short, dry laugh. "You sound just like her. Always chasing meaning in places that never had any."

The table fell quiet. Even the servants paused.

Nisrine's voice dropped. "So what happened to her?"

Lonan rose slowly, hands resting on the carved arms of this chair at the head of the table. "You speak of her like she was the sun. But she wasn't, Nisrine. She was a compromise. An alliance. Useful, once."

18

Nisrine blinked. "Are you saying your marriage was an arrangement?"

He shrugged, casual. "As most royal unions are. She played her part. Until she stopped."

"Stopped?" Her breath caught.

He tilted his head slightly, eyes gleaming with something too smooth to be grief. "She grew disobedient. Started asking the wrong questions. Opening old doors. You'd do well not to follow her example, Princess."

Her blood turned cold. She said softly, "You sound like you know exactly what happened to her."

Lonan smiled but it didn't touch his eyes. "I know enough to say you should let the past rest. She made her choices. And she's gone. That's the only truth worth holding."

He turned, brushing invisible dust from his cloak, and walked away without another glance.

Nisrine remained seated, the clinking of silver and murmurs of court felt suddenly distant, muffled, like sound beneath water.

Her gaze lingered on the place he had stood, the echo of his last words twisting in her mind. *She made her choices. And she's gone.*

A tremor passed through her chest, not fear exactly, but the cold hush that comes before something breaks. Not just what he said, but how he said it. Too calm. Too final. Like a man who didn't lose something, but discarded it. And then she understood.

The realization settled in her chest like a stone dropped in deep water. She pushed her plate away, no longer hungry.

She rose without a word, skirts whispering over the marble as she slipped out of the room and into the cool hush of the corridor. Her footsteps carried her without direction, just away.

Seren found her outside, beneath the twisted silverwood tree that had stood since before the court was built. The early light of morning had barely broken through the branches, as the long shadows stretched across the stones.

Nisrine didn't turn when she heard him. She only spoke, her voice a whisper.

"I don't belong here," she murmured, almost to herself. "This place feels... wrong. I used to feel safe here."

Seren stepped closer. "You don't now?"

Nisrine shook her head again, slower this time. "I know she's still out there. Somewhere. No one will even speak her name anymore. What would happen if I'm next to vanish?"

He didn't need to ask who she meant. His voice dropped, steady and sure. "Your mother."

Nisrine nodded. "Every instinct I have tells me she's alive, Seren. That if I just could get close enough, if I just *look*, I'll find something. But all anyone here wants is for me to forget because my father makes them fear her name."

Seren's jaw worked for a moment like he might argue, but instead he stepped closer. "What do *you* want?"

"To go," she whispered. "I need to see everything for myself and find answers."

Seren stared at her without saying a word. The silence said enough.

Nisrine looked away, and for a moment, her mind slipped backward. Beyond the cold stone of the corridor, past the walls of the palace, to a late summer afternoon, years ago.

They'd been in the orchard where the trees grew crooked and wild, and the guards rarely patrolled. She was seventeen, barefoot and sitting in the long grass, fuming over her upcoming royal trials and her father telling her she had better pass them. Or else.

Seren had tried to cheer her up with clumsy sword tricks and stolen honey cakes, but her heart still ached from her father's harsh words.

"I wish I could just leave," she had muttered, arms around her knees.

"You're not going to," Seren had said confidently, flopping down beside her. "You're going to be Queen someday. And I'll guard your throne."

She had smiled faintly, then hesitated. "Close your eyes," she said.

He did, trusting her without question.

When he opened them, she was holding a delicate thread of green and slender silver chain, a small charm no larger than a fingernail dangling from it. Simple, carved bone with two tiny runes etched into either side.

"My mother gave this to me when I was little," she'd said, the words quiet with reverence. "She told me it meant trust. That when you gave it to someone, it meant your life was safe in their hands."

Seren blinked. "You're giving it to me?"

"I'm giving it to the person I trust most," she'd replied.

21

Then, without ceremony, she'd pricked her finger on a thorn and pressed the charm to the blood. He'd followed suit without flinching, their joined blood sealing the charm in quiet, ancient magic.

"You have to keep it," she'd told him solemnly. "Always. No matter what happens."

"I will," he said, tucking it under his collar like a secret meant only for them.

The memory drifted back into the corners of her mind. A thread still tied, a promise still pulsing.

With a quiet sigh, she retreated back inside to the only bedroom she had ever known. The room was alive with magic. Silken drapes of silver and lavender shifted as though stirred by a breeze. Floating lanterns cast a warm, flickering glow, their light dancing across plush rugs that changed patterns as she moved.

At the center stood her grand four-poster bed, its ancient oak frame etched with protective symbols. Opalescent fabrics draped over it, shimmering with every movement, while enchanted pillows embroidered with celestial patterns were stacked neatly at the head.

Against one wall, a silver-framed mirror adorned her obsidian vanity, the vines curling as if they had grown naturally into shape. Crystal vials of perfume and potions lined its surface, their contents glowing faintly in the dim light. Nearby, her wardrobe stood tall, its carved doors depicting Fae myths, tales of forgotten realms, and celestial dances. Inside, gowns woven from moon thread and enchanted silk shifted colors like the sky at dawn, their magic allowing her to move as effortlessly as the wind.

She drifted toward the balcony, where glowing flowers bloomed in her presence, their fragrance thick with nostalgia. From here, she could see the kingdom stretched out beneath her, the lights of the city twinkling like stars, the land humming with the magic that bound them all together.

Nisrine exhaled slowly, as if the gravity of her thoughts dragged the breath from her. Somewhere beyond these borders lay the answers she sought. And soon, she would find them.

As the laughter in the halls faded and the castle settled into silence, Nisrine made her decision. The kingdom had protected her since birth, but the time had come to leave its embrace.

The human world, wild, untamed, and filled with unknowns, had always been a whisper in her mind, a curiosity she could never shake. Her mother's stories of vast lands and raw emotions lingered in her thoughts. What would it be like to walk among them? To see their world through her own eyes? Could Cherith be among them?

An old memory flooded Nisrine's mind. She smiled faintly as she remembered.

Nisrine had been no older than eight when she first asked her mother about the humans. Not in the way the elders did, with caution and scorn, but with genuine curiosity.

They had been in the palace garden, tucked beneath the boughs of an ancient birch tree. The sun filtered through the leaves in golden shafts, lighting the edges of Queen Cherith's copper-toned hair like fire. Her wings shimmered faintly behind her, delicate and translucent, like panes of glass. She was weaving flower crowns, one for herself, one for Nisrine, and humming a tune that Nisrine didn't recognize.

"Mother," Nisrine asked, fiddling with a strand of ivy, "what are humans really like?"

Cherith glanced at her with a gentle smile. "Curious. Flawed. Brave in their own way. Like us, more than they know."

"But everyone says they're dangerous."

"They can be," her mother replied. "But danger often grows from fear. And fear, my love, is born of misunderstanding."

Nisrine frowned, unsure how to make sense of that. "But why do we stay hidden, then? Why not just… talk to them?"

Cherith set down the half-finished crown in her lap and turned to face her fully. "Because too many have forgotten who we are. They see magic as something to conquer, not to understand. But it wasn't always like this."

"You've seen it? When Fae and humans lived together?"

Her mother's eyes turned wistful. "I have. There were once villages where humans and Fae shared harvests. They exchanged stories around the fire. Some even fell in love."

Nisrine's eyes widened. "Really?"

Cherith chuckled softly. "Yes. And sometimes it ended badly. But sometimes… it was beautiful."

They sat in silence for a while, the wind rustling the leaves above them. Then her mother leaned in closer, voice lowered. "The truth, Nisrine, is that the stories the elders tell are only part of the truth. We must remember the rest. That's why I study the old texts, why I keep the stories alive. One day, you'll have to decide what to do with them."

That memory had stayed with Nisrine for years, long after her mother vanished. Even now, it burned bright in her mind, the softness of her voice, the smell of lavender and ink on her robes, and the way she had looked at Nisrine as though she already knew her daughter would one day walk the line between two worlds.

With quiet resolve, she crossed the room, running her fingers over the carved doors of her wardrobe. Gowns of silk and stardust hung within, but they belonged to the life she was leaving behind. Instead, she reached for a cloak woven from twilight's shadows, its fabric weightless yet strong enough to mask her presence. As she fastened the silver clasp at her throat, her wings fluttered softly, brushing against the fabric in a quiet farewell.

A breeze stirred through the balcony, sending a shiver through her. The night called to her like an unspoken promise, the cool wind weaving through the trees as if urging her forward.

She stepped onto the stone ledge, the kingdom stretching below like a tapestry of light and shadow. The magic in the air pulsed with her heartbeat, the hush of the world before her charged with anticipation. She spread her wings, lavender and jade catching the moonlight, and with one last glance at the only home she had ever known, she took flight.

The castle faded behind her. The world ahead was vast, unknown, and waiting.

And with every beat of her wings, she soared toward it.

Chapter 3

Nisrine took a deep breath. The cool air of the forest filled her lungs. As she passed the pond, the water's shimmering surface still rippled from the subtle magic she'd earlier stirred. Her eyebrows furrowed, seeing it still moving. She paused to stand by the water's edge. "Was that me or someone else?" She thought out loud. She looked around, but nothing moved. Every second spent here was another second she delayed what she had already decided to do.

Her gaze turned toward the ancient oaks that loomed like silent sentinels, their twisted roots gripping the earth like the very veins of the world. There, hidden deep in the forest, lay the

Fae Gate, the only portal that connected her world to the human realm. It was a place shrouded in mystery, known to few, and even fewer dared to cross its threshold.

But Nisrine was different. She had been dreaming of this moment for years. A small smile crossed her mouth as she remembered daydreaming aloud with her mother about this very moment. Her heart raced with excitement.

With a flutter of her wings, she flew into the air, lifting above the ground as though the wind itself was urging her onward. The forest felt alive beneath her, the trees shifting in response to her movements, their branches whispering softly in a language she almost understood. The ancient magic of the land hummed with an energy she could feel deep in her bones.

The Fae Gate was not far, hidden by thick, tangled vines and enchanted with a spell that made it almost impossible for those who were unworthy, or uninvited, to see. She followed the invisible yet visible path, winding through the forest, the air thick with the scent of moss and damp earth.

As she neared the clearing where the gate lay, the air grew colder, and an unnatural stillness settled over the forest. Overhead, the moon bathed the glade in an eerie silver glow, illuminating the gate, a towering archway of gnarled branches, twisted and woven like the bones of the forest itself. Between the interlocking limbs, a faint golden light pulsed, steady and rhythmic, like the heartbeat of something ancient and alive. This was no ordinary structure. The gate was a living entity, forged from the essence of the Fae, its form ever-shifting, evolving with the dim, whispering magic that surrounded it.

Nisrine stopped before it, her pulse quickening. Slowly, she pushed back the hood of her cloak, her gaze locked on the undulating glow before her.

A voice, quiet yet firm, broke the silence. "Are you sure, Princess?"

She turned sharply. From the shadows emerged a tall figure, his aqua eyes gleaming in the moonlight. Seren. He stood with the stillness of someone bracing for a storm.

"You're going alone?" His voice was low, almost pleading. "The humans… What if they are not what you believe them to be? What if you…"

"I have to, Seren." She cut him off, her voice steady, though the ache in her chest threatened to splinter her calm. "I need to know what's out there. If my mother crossed through… I can't stay here and wonder."

Seren took a step forward, his expression dark with worry. "The gate is not meant to be used lightly. It's ancient and unpredictable. If you leave, the forest will change. Your wings will remain here, in this realm. The balance will fall."

"I know." Her gaze softened, but her resolve did not waver. "But I cannot spend my life wondering. I need to see for myself what's real. What we were never told."

His hands clenched at his sides. His voice was sharper now, laced with something dangerously close to desperation. "What if you go through that gate and find nothing but ruin? You don't know what's waiting for you, Nisrine. None of us do."

She smiled faintly, eyes burning. "I have to find out."

He exhaled sharply, shaking his head. "I can't let you go. Hell, you've never even held a sword! How are you going to protect yourself?"

Nisrine's heart clenched, but she lifted her chin, stepping closer. "You don't have a choice, Seren. I will be careful."

For a moment, he looked as if he might try to stop her. His muscles tensed, his wings twitched as if preparing to block her path. But something in her gaze made him falter. He knew her too well. She had already made up her mind.

His jaw tightened. "Damn it, Nis," he muttered, his voice low.

His voice stirred something old inside her, something long buried.

A memory surfaced, unbidden but vivid: she and Seren, no more than children, racing through the twilight-drenched fields of moonlilies behind the palace. Their wings, smaller then, beat with playful urgency as they leapt and tumbled through the soft grass.

Nisrine had hit a tree and tumbled to the ground, skinning her knee, and sat there blinking back tears when Seren landed beside her in a flurry of awkward limbs and puffed-up pride. He was always trying to impress her, even then.

"You're supposed to watch where you're flying," he had said seriously, brushing a leaf from her hair.

She scowled. "You were supposed to catch me."

He looked horrified by his failure and had immediately offered his hand. "I will next time. I promise."

She took it, as she always did, and together they sat watching the fireflies blink to life above the silvergrass.

"Do you think the human stories are true?" she had asked, her voice hushed, as if the trees themselves might overhear.

He had frowned. "Which ones?"

"The ones where they're not all bad. Where they help Fae. Where they fall in love with stars."

Seren had rolled his eyes dramatically. "That's just old fluff. My brother says humans only want what they can't control."

"But maybe they're just scared. Like we are." She looked up at the sky, then at him. "Maybe someone just needs to be brave first."

Even then, he hadn't argued with her. He never did when she got that look in her eyes. Instead, he'd taken a twig and drawn a shaky star in the dirt between them.

"If you go looking for them," he said, "I'll follow you. I'll protect you."

Nisrine remembered laughing, reaching out to press her hand over his. "You always say that."

"I always mean it," he replied.

The memory faded, but it didn't let go.

Nisrine stood straighter, her heart pulled by the echoes of what had been. "You once said you'd follow me," she said softly, not as a challenge, but as a memory.

Seren's jaw clenched. "And I would," he said. "You know I would."

"I do." Her voice trembled, just barely, but she didn't look away. "But if anyone goes with me, it'll look like the start of an invasion. The humans already fear the Fae. If I show up with a guard at my side, they'll see me as a threat."

Seren was silent for a long moment. Then, almost too quietly, he said, "I could go as something else."

Her heart sank, the meaning behind his words deeper than his voice revealed. She turned toward him fully. "I know," she whispered. "Not now. If I let myself feel that right now, I might never leave."

Seren didn't answer. He just stared at her; his eyes clouded with something unreadable. His expression faltered. His throat bobbed with a swallow. And in that silence, something shifted.

Before he could find the words, before he could stop her, she turned and stepped through the gate.

The moment she was gone, the clearing fell silent. The air where she had stood was suddenly too empty, too still. And then, as his gaze fell to the ground, he gasped.

Seren stood frozen, his gaze fixed on the spot where she had disappeared. The pulse of magic still lingered in the air, sharp and raw, but the space where she had stood was now empty. He hadn't been able to stop her. He hadn't even tried, not truly. But the consequences of the decision wrapped around him, and the sharp fear that gripped him was something he could not ignore. He had known, from the start, that she would go. But knowing it and watching her disappear into that unknown world were two entirely different things.

His feet moved before his mind could catch up. He knelt slowly, his heart heavy in his chest, as his eyes fell on the ground before him. There, where Nisrine had stood, lay her wings glowing softly in the moonlight. They lay perfectly still, abandoned in the wake of her disappearance. For a long moment, Seren simply knelt there, what had just happened rooting itself in his bones. The wings, now motionless and lifeless without her, seemed impossibly small.

Seren reached for the wings, his hands trembling slightly. For a long moment, he simply held them, feeling the ache of the loss, the hollowness she'd left behind.

He didn't move right away. The gate still flickered, magic dissolving into the forest air like the last breath of a dream. Only when the breeze shifted, colder and emptier now, did Seren turn toward the path home.

The walk was long and heavy. Each step felt like trudging through quicksand, the crushing pull of duty, heavy enough to smother. Leaves whispered above him, low and mournful, as though the forest already knew what Nisrine had done.

He passed through the outer gates without a word, his face unreadable, arms still wrapped protectively around the folded iridescent wings. The sentries glanced at him but said nothing. He was Royal Guard after all. Unquestioned. Unchallenged.

Until he entered the inner corridor.

On Fallen Wings

His commanding officer, Captain Veyric, stood near the marble archway, speaking with two lower-ranked guards. His voice stilled as he turned. His eyes landed on what Seren held. Silence fell like a blade. Seren tried to turn around but it was too late.

"Seren," Veyric said, slowly stepping forward. "What... is that?"

Seren didn't answer immediately.

Veyric's mouth opened. "Why do you have the princess's wings?"

"She made a choice," Seren said quietly, "One I couldn't stop."

The Captain's gaze sharpened.

"You're coming with me." He grabbed Seren's arm and pulled him forward.

Captain Veyric dragged him to King Lonan's chamber, Seren's arms still cradling the wings carefully.

The door creaked open and Lonan turned from the hearth, his expression already darkening. "What is this?"

Seren's voice was low, steady. "She's gone."

The words hung in the air like a curse.

The king's breath hitched as his sharp eyes locked onto Seren's. He looked down at what Seren held, the fragile remnants of his daughter. For a moment, he said nothing. Silence pressed thick and suffocating between them.

"She... went through?" His voice was hoarse, barely above a whisper. "Alone?"

Seren swallowed hard and nodded. "She did." He exhaled sharply. "And now... we must face what comes next."

King Lonan's gaze lingered on the wings, his fingers twitching as if resisting the urge to reach for them. A shadow passed over his face, something darker than grief. His jaw clenched as he forced himself to look away.

Chapter 4

The High Court of Constalatia had never felt so still.

It was usually a place of murmured debate and rustling silks, of music filtering through stained glass and Fae magic gently humming through the marble columns. The chamber now held only silence, and the low, uneven breath of a king whose world had just changed.

Seren stood motionless in the center of the room. The wings still rested in his arms, carefully cradled as though they might vanish if he blinked. Around him, the courtiers had gathered in uneasy clusters, faces pale, expressions tight. Whispers flickered like ghostlight through the hall, but no one dared raise their voice.

King Lonan sat upon his Throne of Thorns, its twisted silver thorned branches curling high behind him. His shoulders sagged slightly due to his age, his eyes were sharp, dark with disbelief and fury.

"You let her go." His voice was quiet. Too quiet. "You stood at the gate and let my daughter pass into the human world... chasing a ghost."

Seren's throat tightened. "I tried to stop her."

"No," Lonan said, cutting through his words like a blade. "You didn't."

The accusation hung in the air like a storm cloud about to break.

Seren met it without a word, jaw set, eyes steady. What would he say? He had known this would come, the blame and the fury. He was her protector. Her oldest friend. And he had let her go.

"She was determined," Seren said at last, his voice rough. "She believes Cherith may still be out there. That her disappearance wasn't chance. That someone..."

"Enough," Lonan growled. His hands clinched the arms of his throne, knuckles white. "She's chasing shadows. There is no 'out there.' Only danger. Only ruin."

Someone at the edge of the chamber whispered, "She thinks her mother was taken."

Lonan turned sharply, his silver beard bristling, eyes flashing with something colder than rage. "Then she is a fool." The words echoed through the hall, final and unforgiving.

Seren's jaw tightened the way a bowstring does before it snaps, but he didn't look away. "She left knowing her wings would remain and she'd never fly again. That wasn't foolishness. That was sacrifice. That was intent."

"It means she is gone," Lonan said, standing slowly. "Gone chasing lies better left buried. The only of my line, and she casts aside her duty for ghosts."

His gaze snapped to Seren. "You knew what she was planning and you let her go."

"Yes. She deserves the truth."

Silence bloomed again.

Lonan descended the steps from his throne, each movement deliberate. He stopped inches before Seren, looking down at the wings in his soldier's arms. "She is everything we have left."

"I know."

"She trusted you."

"I know."

For a moment, it looked as if the king might strike him. But then his hands fell to his sides, limp and trembling. "Get out of my sight."

Seren bowed low, deeper than ceremony required. Then he turned and left, each footstep sounding like a tolling bell.

Behind him, the court remained silent. And above them all, the stained-glass windows of Constalatia glinted coldly, depicting a long-forgotten time when the veil between worlds had first been torn, and the cost of crossing it had not yet been forgotten.

Seren's footsteps rang in the silence of the empty halls, the king's words still clinging to him, suffocating, each step a bitter echo of the failure now carved into him. His arms felt heavy with the wings he still cradled, and the air itself seemed too thick, too oppressive, as though the very castle was aware of the tragedy unfolding within its walls.

His mind replayed the moment again and again, each thought as painful as the last.

I tried to stop her.

But the words were hollow, no more than an excuse. He had seen the determination in her eyes, the stubborn set of her jaw as she had made her decision. He had known that no matter how hard he tried, no matter how many arguments or warnings he gave, she would not listen. Nisrine was never one to be swayed by fear. She was driven by something deeper, something that pulsed within her, something that called her toward the unknown.

Why did I think I could change that?

Seren stopped in the middle of the corridor, pressing his palm against the stone wall. The coolness of it did little to ease the heat flooding his chest. His eyes fell to the wings. Nisrine's wings. The delicate, shimmering appendages were now still, lifeless without their owner. They felt like a part of him, like a piece of his own soul, and he couldn't shake the sense of failure that clung to him like a second skin.

He had sworn to protect her. To keep her safe.

But now, she was gone, and all that remained were these fragile wings, a physical reminder of the promises he'd failed to keep.

A voice, low, almost a whisper, seemed to echo through the empty halls. *You were supposed to protect her.*

His heart twisted in his chest.

38

On Fallen Wings

Seren's thoughts were interrupted as he reached his chambers. The door swung open without resistance, and he stepped inside, his boots clicking softly against the marble floor. The room was dim, the heavy velvet curtains drawn tight against the light. The air smelled faintly of incense, a remnant from the last time he'd had company, a time that felt as distant as another life.

The familiar weight of the wings in his hands didn't make him feel better. It only made him feel hollow.

He walked to the fireplace and set the wings on the stone mantle. For a moment, he simply stood there, staring at them. The fire crackled softly, casting shadows that danced across the stone walls. A bitter laugh escaped him. How useless it all seemed. His duty. His oaths. His failure.

Seren's fingers ran over the edge of the wings, tracing the intricate patterns that had once shimmered with life. A deep, aching sadness filled him as his mind wandered back to the days when everything had been simpler. When he and Nisrine were children, and the world had felt like a place of endless possibility.

He remembered those carefree days so clearly, chasing each other through the palace gardens, laughing until they could hardly breathe, daring each other to race to the top of the highest tower. He could still hear her laughter, light and full of mischief, echoing through the halls. They had been inseparable back then, two notes in the same chord. She had been his best friend, his sidekick, and in a way, he had been hers.

But somewhere along the way, everything had changed. Seren scrubbed at his face, his eyes squeezed shut. *How did we get here?*

The day she had first begun speaking of humans had been the day he had realized how much the world had shifted. He had seen the glimmer of something in her eyes. A desire to to break free from her fathers reign and to find her lost mother.

And when she had asked him, in that quiet, earnest voice, if she could go through the gate, if she could cross into the human world, he had known then that the choice had been made.

"Please," she had whispered, "don't make me stay here. I need to know. I need to find the truth."

He had tried to reason with her. He had warned her of the dangers. But nothing had been enough. Nisrine had been determined. When she had made up her mind, nothing, no force in the world, could have stopped her.

Not even him.

And so here he was now, standing in the silence of his chambers, grappling with the consequences of his inaction. *Why didn't I try harder? Why didn't I just…*

His thoughts were interrupted by a soft knock on the door.

He turned toward it, his heart sinking. No doubt it was one of the courtiers, perhaps one of the king's advisors, wanting to know what happened. Or perhaps the king himself, coming to berate him again.

But when the door opened it was Olesia, Princess Nisrine's lady-in-waiting.

Her eyes were heavy with unspoken understanding as she stepped inside, her expression darkened by the same guilt that clung to him. She closed the door softly behind her, and for a moment, neither of them spoke.

On Fallen Wings

Seren took a deep breath, his chest tightening. "Olesia… you knew. You knew she was going to leave, didn't you?"

Olesia nodded, her face a mixture of sorrow and resignation. "I did." Her voice was soft, but there was no avoiding the truth in her words. "She had been talking about it for weeks. About her mother, about the gate… she couldn't let it go."

"Why didn't you stop her?" The question was out of his mouth before he could think better of it. He regretted it immediately, but it was too late. His anger, his pain, his guilt, everything poured out in a single question. He had wanted to protect her. To protect Nisrine. He had wanted to stop her from making this mistake.

Olesia's eyes softened, and she took a step closer to him. "I couldn't stop her either, Seren. No one could."

"I should have," Seren muttered, his voice barely above a whisper. "I swore I'd protect her. I failed."

Olesia's expression hardened. "No. You didn't fail. You can't control what's inside of her. She made her choice. She's always made her own path, Seren."

He turned away, unable to meet her gaze. "I should have done something. Anything."

"You did what you could. But it was never going to be enough." Olesia's voice was firm now, steady. "Nisrine is not a child anymore. She's a princess carrying the burden of the realm with every step. And you… You can't protect her from everything. Sometimes, you have to let them go. Even if it breaks you."

Seren's chest tightened painfully at her words. He had always known that Nisrine was destined for something greater. But knowing and accepting it were two entirely different things.

Olesia placed a hand on his shoulder, offering him a silent comfort. They stood there for a long moment, the silence between them thick with shared grief.

Eventually, Seren spoke again, his voice barely audible. "What happens now?"

Olesia exhaled slowly. "Now, we wait. We wait and see if she comes back. And if not... we go after her."

The words were simple. Direct. But they sank into Seren's chest like a stone.

It was time to face what had been set in motion. Time to face the consequences of Nisrine's choice. And his own.

Chapter 5

Colors bled into each other in ways that defied nature, twisting into dizzying patterns that seemed to tug at the mind. For a moment, it was as if the universe itself had unraveled, exposing realms beyond comprehension. Within the vortex, glimpses of distant worlds flickered, blurred, shifting landscapes that felt both familiar and utterly alien, where time was a suggestion, gravity a fleeting notion, and reality itself seemed malleable.

The air around Nisrine hummed with a soft, melodic resonance, as though the stars themselves were singing. It was a sound that reverberated deep within, echoing not only in her ears but in the very heart of her being. The wind that swirled around it carried the scent of wildflowers, mingling with the sharp sweetness of untamed magic and the rich, grounding scent of the forest. The energy in the air was palpable, thick with a presence both alluring and dangerous, like the promise of something impossible yet inevitable. It was as if the gate were alive, a living dream, waiting patiently for her to step beyond.

As Nisrine stepped through, the world around her folded into a blur of light and shadow, leaving nothing but a stillness behind. The soft hum of the gate faded into the night, and the clearing grew eerily silent, save for the faint rustle of the wind through the trees.

The world beyond the Fae Gate was nothing like what Nisrine had imagined. The forest, still lush and vibrant, felt different, denser somehow, as if it bore the memory of a thousand years in every leaf and branch. The air had an unfamiliar tang to it, a sharpness that stung her nose. It wasn't the clean, crisp scent of her kingdom. And there, in the distance, she could make out shapes moving. At first, they seemed like shadows, but as she focused, she saw the outlines of what looked like houses, rudimentary structures, crafted from wood and stone, with strange flickering lights inside. The sounds of movement reached her ears: the distant murmur of voices, the clang of metal against metal, and something else, too, a kind of deep, unsettling hum, like the pulse of the earth itself.

The human world.

Nisrine took a cautious step forward, her heart pounding with both fear and excitement. She had crossed the threshold. There was no turning back now.

And somewhere, hidden deep within this world, was the truth she had longed to find.

She took another step as she carefully surveyed her surroundings. The trees around her were ancient, but their bark was rougher, more gnarled, and their branches stretched out in strange, jagged patterns. The ground was softer underfoot, as if the earth here was not quite as solid as the soil in her world.

It felt... wrong. Yet, Nisrine pressed on, determined not to let fear take root.

Then she felt it.

A strange lightness. A hollow absence.

Her breath hitched. She reached behind her instinctively, her fingers searching for the familiar softness of her wings. But there was nothing. Just air.

Panic surged through her as she twisted, trying to see, to feel. Her hands ran over her back, her shoulders, where her wings should have been, where they had always been. But they were gone.

She sucked in a sharp breath, her heart hammering. The gate had taken them. Just as Seren had warned.

A shiver ran down her spine, but she gritted her teeth and forced herself to steady her breathing. It was too late to turn back now.

A flicker of magic sparked in her palm. It was weaker than she expected. Hesitant, as if the power itself was unfamiliar with this new world.

She forced herself to focus, drawing a faint glow forward. The light hovered, trembling like a candle flame in a draft, and reached a nearby tree. The rough bark shimmered faintly beneath the flow, and a few brittle leaves stirred as if woken by her breath.

A faint pressure tugged at her senses, as if something unseen had taken notice.

"Is anyone there?" she called out softly, her voice cutting through the strange, quiet stillness.

No answer.

Then, from somewhere beyond the trees, a quiet voice drifted in, casual, almost amused. "That depends. Are you planning to collapse the rest of the forest with your landing? You're lucky I was nearby and heard the commotion. Magic like that doesn't happen often. Too loud. Too… bright."

A tall figure stepped from the trees, his dark worn coat blending with the night. His hood was pushed back enough to reveal tangled light brown hair and eyes that watched Nisrine with quiet curiosity.

"You're not from here," he said, his voice gruff and cautious. "Which makes you either very brave or very stupid." His eyes darted to her pointed ears for a moment, narrowing, then quickly flicking back to her face. "What are you?"

Nisrine swallowed, taking a step forward, her heart racing with a mix of excitement and trepidation. She had come this far, and she couldn't afford to hesitate now.

"I'm… a traveler," she said, her voice steady, though a strange tightness had formed in her throat. She wasn't sure what to say… *a princess?* How would that go over in this world? "I come from… beyond the forest."

The man raised an eyebrow, clearly unconvinced. "Beyond the forest?" he repeated, his tone skeptical. "The *other* side of the barrier?"

Nisrine nodded, unsure whether to reveal too much too soon. "Yes. I... I'm looking for someone. I need to know more about this world. About the humans."

The man's expression shifted, a flicker of recognition passing over his features before he quickly masked it. "Humans, eh?"

The way he spoke the word *humans* sent another shiver down her spine. But there was no time to dwell on that. She needed to understand who he was.

"I—" Nisrine began, but her words faltered as something caught her attention, a glimmer of movement in the trees behind the man. Another figure, cloaked in shadow, was watching them from a distance. Nisrine's instincts flared, the old, primal magic within her rising in response.

"Who else is there?" she asked sharply, her eyes narrowing.

The man turned, his posture suddenly defensive, his hand brushing the hilt of a blade she hadn't noticed before. "It's not what you think. You're not the first to come through here. Granted... it's been awhile since anyone came through the way you just did." His gaze flicked back to her ears. "I know what you are. Fae, aren't you?"

Nisrine nodded slowly. "I am. My name is Nisrine. But I'm not here to cause harm. I just need answers."

The man raised a brow, a crooked smile tugging at his lips. Nisrine noticed his teeth looked very different from hers. They appeared longer. Sharper. "Well, that's new," he said, voice smooth with amusement. "Most people who come stumbling through the trees with that look on their face are either lost or looking for a fight." His golden eyes flicked over

47

her, sharp and calculating, but not unkind. "Which one are you?"

"I'm looking for the truth," she replied.

The man let out a soft laugh, more incredulous than mocking. "She wants *the truth*, Elaila. Shall we just hand it over?"

A second figure stepped into view from the trees, a woman with piercing eyes and movements so fluid they barely disturbed the undergrowth. She said nothing at first, only studied Nisrine with a tilt of her head, like someone inspecting a puzzle that shouldn't exist.

"She's not lying," the woman said at last, her voice cool.

"I'm standing right here," Nisrine said, a bit more sharply than she intended.

"We noticed," the man said, grinning now. "I'm Dade, by the way. This is Elaila. She usually lets me do the talking until I've said something reckless."

"You're about three words away," Elaila murmured.

Dade's grin widened.

Elaila stepped closer, her gaze still locked on Nisrine. "You crossed the barrier alone?"

Nisrine hesitated, then nodded. "Yes."

"And you left your wings behind," Elaila said, more to herself than to anyone else.

"That takes some balls. Or desperation." Dade added.

Nisrine met his gaze. "I need to find someone. My mother. She disappeared years ago and I think she might be on this side of the barrier."

That seemed to shift something. Dade's posture eased just slightly. Elaila's eyes narrowed, not in suspicion, but in thought.

"Fae don't just end up over here," Elaila said. "Not without cost. Or cause."

"Which is why I need answers," Nisrine said. "No one in my realm will talk about what happened. And now that I'm here…" Her voice faltered, but she steadied herself. "I can feel it. Something's wrong. The magic. The air. Like the world is waiting for something to break."

Before anyone could say anything else, the air around them seemed to thicken, the temperature dropping suddenly. A low hum reverberated through the ground beneath her feet, and the trees around them began to shift, as if alive with an energy of their own. Something was changing.

Dade's smile faded entirely. "You're not wrong."

Elaila folded her arms. "Come with us. We can talk more at our camp. It's safer there."

Nisrine hesitated. "Why help me?"

Dade shrugged. "You haven't tried to stab us yet. And Elaila's right, you don't seem like a liar."

"And," Elaila added, glancing into the trees, "if you're really telling the truth, then you've stepped into something much larger than you know."

Dade smirked and said, "Besides, it's been a while since anything interesting happened around here."

Nisrine didn't move at first. Her gaze shifted to the clearing behind her where the gate had once shimmered. But now it was dull as if all the magic was used up sending her here.

She swallowed. "There's no way back… is there?" she asked, almost to herself.

"Not tonight," Elaila answered.

Nisrine's fingers curled at her sides. She didn't trust them, not yet, but there was something careful in Elaila's tone. Something that didn't feel like a threat. They were strange, yes. But she had just crossed into a world filled with unknowns.

"I'll come," she said finally, wary but resolved.

Elaila gave a nod. Dade spun lightly on his heel, already leading the way through the trees.

He moved like he belonged to the shadows, slipping through the dim underbrush with an ease that made it hard to tell where darkness ended and he began.

The clearing faded behind them. And with it, any illusion of going back.

The dense forest was alive with the sounds of the evening, crickets chirping with the rustling of leaves, the soft call of distant birds, and the occasional crack of a twig breaking underfoot. Amidst the towering trees, a camp had appeared, nestled nicely, its presence as natural as the land itself. The heart of the camp was a large fire pit, surrounded by a ring of smooth stones. Its flames flickered and danced, casting long shadows against the trunks of ancient oaks and pines. Smoke floated lazily into the air, dissipating into the scent of burning pinewood, the fragrance mingling with the damp earth of the forest.

Elaila sat on a rock furthest away from the fire. Dade positioned himself behind her, standing and guarding. She motioned openly for Nisrine to choose a place to sit. Nisrine caught herself staring at Elaila. She was unnaturally beautiful, and the way the firelight danced across her face seemed to make her eyes change colors between golds and reds. And her teeth were almost identical to Dade's.

Nisrine sat on a log closest to the fire. She drew her knees closer, the warmth of the fire barely cutting through the chill settling in her bones. It was far colder here than in her kingdom. Her gaze flicked between Elaila and Dade, both too still, too composed as if they weren't just expecting danger, but had lived with it for centuries.

She spoke quietly. "My mother disappeared. No one talks about it. Not my father. Not the court. Just silence. Like pretending it never happened will make it true."

Elaila tilted her head, eyes narrowing slightly. "Queen Cherith," she said, as if testing the weight of the name on her tongue. "That's who you're looking for?"

Nisrine's breath caught. "How do you know her name?"

Elaila didn't answer immediately. Instead, she stood, slow and graceful, her cloak shifting like liquid shadow around her. She stepped to the edge of the firelight, her gaze fixed on something in the dark. "Because names like that don't vanish," she said finally. "Not really. Not when they've touched the magic the way she did."

Dade crossed his arms, his tone quieter now. "We heard whispers. Years ago. Rumors of a Fae queen who crossed through and never returned."

Nisrine's heart stuttered. "She was here?"

Dade stepped forward as he handed Nisrine some food. She hadn't even noticed he had moved to fetch it.

"No one knows for certain," Elaila replied, glancing back at her. "But the magic here remembers. If she came through… the land would know."

Dade dropped into a crouch beside her, his usual sharpness edged with something more serious. "Why now, Nisrine? Why risk coming through after all this time?"

"Because I think my father lied." she said, the words tumbling out faster than she expected. "He told me to forget her. That she made her choice. But I saw something in his eyes when I asked again. Not grief. Guilt."

That caught Elaila's attention. She turned fully, watching Nisrine in the firelight, her expression unreadable. She didn't blink.

"You think he had something to do with her disappearance," Elaila said.

"I don't think," Nisrine whispered. "I *know*."

A long silence stretched between them, broken only by the fire's soft crackle and the occasional snap of a log shifting.

A low, mournful howl echoed through the trees. Another followed it, and then another, until the forest itself seemed to respond with a ripple of energy.

Elaila said, her voice lower now. "If your mother crossed over, and if she survived… she wouldn't be the same. Not after all this time."

"I don't care," Nisrine said. "If there's even a chance, I have to try."

Dade signed, standing again and pacing a few steps toward the edge of the camp. "You're walking in deep waters, girl. Waters your mother might have drowned in."

"But maybe she didn't," Nisrine said, sitting up taller. "Maybe she's still out there. Maybe she's waiting."

Elaila studied her for a long moment. Then, to Nisrine's surprise, she nodded. "Then we'll help you search. If she's out there... but you need to understand something first."

Nisrine waited, her breath held.

"If you follow this path," Elaila continued, "you won't be able to return unchanged. You'll find answers. But not all of them will be kind."

Dade's voice cut in, softer. "And some truths... want to stay buried."

Chapter 6

Later, once the fire had burned lower and the night wrapped itself around the camp in quiet stillness, Dade plopped himself down beside Nisrine with exaggerated exhaustion. "Well, I think we've earned a bit of light conversation. Don't you think, Elaila?" Dade said, staring into the embers.

Elaila didn't glance at him. She sat rigid, sharpening a blade that looked far too old to be human-forged. "Light conversation is for fools who think the night won't find them."

Dade leaned toward Nisrine with a mock whisper. "She's an absolute delight at dinner parties."

Though something ached deep inside her, Nisrine managed a faint smile. "You two have been traveling together long?"

Dade stretched his legs out, folding his hands behind his head. "A few decades, give or take. Long enough for her to almost laugh at my jokes."

"I've never laughed at your jokes," Elaila said without looking up.

"She chuckled once," Dade insisted. "Seven years ago. You remember it, don't you?"

"I was coughing," Elaila said.

Nisrine let out a soft laugh, which seemed to surprise even herself. The moment cracked something open in her, easing the edge of the dread that had clung to her since arriving. It felt good to feel like herself again, even if only for a breath.

"How did you meet?" she asked, her voice quiet.

Dade rolled a small twig between his fingers. "We were both hunting the same beast. It was killing villagers, and the local lord put a bounty on its head. We arrived in the same town, glared at each other from opposite ends of the tavern, then spent three nights trying to beat the other to the kill."

"I got there first," Elaila added without emotion.

Dade grinned. "Only because I distracted the beast with my charming personality."

Elaila looked at Nisrine with cool unblinking eyes. "He nearly got himself killed. I stepped in."

"Saved by an immortal ice queen," Dade said, grinning. "It was very romantic."

"It was inconvenient," Elaila muttered.

"You stayed," Nisrine observed.

Dade looked at her, eyes flickering with something softer. "Yeah. We make a good team. She's the brains, I'm the charisma."

"You're the risk," Elaila corrected. "But sometimes a necessary one."

They were opposites, Nisrine realized, but they worked together with the kind of ease that only came from time and trust. For a moment, she envied it.

"Why did you help me?" she asked. "Back there. You didn't know me. You could've sent me away."

Elaila's eyes flicked to the shadows beyond the fire. "You carry old magic. It called out when you crossed the barrier. We felt it. Like a ripple under the skin."

"And more importantly," Dade said, "you didn't come through here swinging a sword or throwing spells around. That's rare these days. People usually lead with violence. You led with questions. We figured we'd see how deep your curiosity went before deciding if you were dangerous."

Nisrine looked between them. "And? What do you think now?"

Elaila was quiet for a long moment. "Undecided."

Dade added, "But leaning toward 'interesting.'"

Nisrine pulled her knees up to her chest, the fire warming her skin. "I didn't expect to find... people like you on this side of the barrier."

She tried to put her hand on Elaila's arm to give a light touch to genuinely thank her for her hospitality. Elaila felt the warmth radiating from Nisrine's hand and jerked her arm away. Nisrine thought it was because she didn't know her well enough

On Fallen Wings

to be touched by her, but in the back of her mind, she couldn't help but notice the cold surrounding Elaila.

Dade gave a theatrical bow from where he sat and flicked the twig into the fire. "We're very thoughtful."

Elaila sighed. "You'll rest here tonight. Tomorrow, we'll talk more. There's history you need to hear, truths buried so deep even the Fae have forgotten them."

Nisrine glanced up. "And you'll tell me?"

Elaila's gaze softened ever so slightly. "You came seeking answers. We'll give them. But understand, once you know, there's no undoing it. And it will change how you see your own kind."

Dade poked at the fire with a stick. "You should get some sleep. The world doesn't get kinder tomorrow."

Nisrine nodded slowly. Her limbs ached with a deep, hollow fatigue as she rose and followed Elaila's gesture toward a low, nondescript tent. The flap rustled as she stepped inside, and the scent of canvas and earth replaced the lavender and silk of her former chambers. A rough wool blanket lay folded over a thin bedroll, lumpy and uneven, spread out on the packed dirt floor. She sat slowly, brushing aside a pebble and trying not to grimace. The wool itched against her fingers as she pulled it over her, scratchy and unfamiliar. Around her, the tent sagged slightly, held upright by weathered stakes and sheer necessity. Outside, she could still hear the quiet crackle of firewood, Elaila's voice low and steady, Dade's curling in and out of laughter. For a long moment, Nisrine simply lay still, staring at the canvas above her, the absence of carved ceilings and flowing drapes louder than silence. This was not home. But it was what she had now.

The morning mist clung low to the forest floor, curling around tree roots like smoke. Light filtered through the canvas tent in fractured beams, gilding everything in pale gold. Nisrine stirred beneath the worn wool blanket they'd given her, the air still holding a bite of cold that reminded her she was far from the velvet warmth of the Fae Court.

She sat up slowly. The tent rustled as she pushed aside the flap.

Dade appeared from behind a tree, an apple in hand, and tossed her a grin. "You sleep like someone who's never had to worry about assassins."

"I haven't," she replied dryly, catching the apple he lobbed at her next.

"Well, that ends today. Welcome to the world of being hunted." He sank onto a moss-covered log, sprawling with casual grace. "Do you want breakfast or trauma first?"

Nisrine cleared her throat and looked around. "How long have you been awake?"

Dade gave a lopsided grin. "Let's just say sleep is… optional."

Elaila stood at the edge of the camp, her dark hair swept back, pale skin catching the light like polished stone. Her expression was unreadable, but her eyes held none of the sharp rebuke from the night before. Only a guarded stillness.

Dade made a low sound, a half-snort, half-laugh, as he glanced at Elaila. "Here we go. Trauma it is. Better hope she's feeling poetic today."

"I'm not interested in poetry," Nisrine said softly. "I want the truth."

Elaila's tensed, but after a long pause, she spoke. "There was a war," she said flatly. "Not the kind with banners and declarations. Not at first. It started quietly, rumors, strange disappearances, pockets of wild magic where the veil between realms had already begun to thin."

She finally turned her gaze to Nisrine. "It wasn't just humans trying to use magic. It was Fae who gave it to them. Carelessly. Curiously. Some thought they were helping. Others thought they were… experimenting."

Dade added, "You ever seen a mortal body try to hold pure magic? Doesn't end well. Bones snap. Blood boils. And the ones who survive? They go mad… or worse."

Elaila's tone was colder now. "And when things spiraled out of control, when entire cities were consumed by what they didn't understand, the humans begged for the Fae to fix it. To seal it away."

Nisrine stared into the fire. "So, the Fae created the barrier?"

"Yes," Elaila said directly.

Dade made a face. "Not everyone agreed, of course. Some Fae fought to stay. Others… they vanished before the sealing began."

"Your mother," Elaila added suddenly, and Nisrine looked up sharply. "Queen Cherith. She was there. That's why she was studying it. But then she disappeared."

Nisrine's heart leapt into her throat. "You knew her?"

"I knew *of* her," Elaila said with a shrug. "She was a diplomat. One of the few Fae who tried to understand both sides. Some say she believed the barrier would be temporary. That balance could be restored."

"And now?" Nisrine asked.

Elaila's face darkened again. "Now the balance is broken. The humans have forgotten the truth. The Fae have forgotten the cost. And if something happens to the barrier, if magic comes back in the way it once was…"

Dade finished for her. "It won't be a reunion. It'll be a reckoning."

For a moment, the only sound was the soft hiss of pine sap popping in the fire. Then Dade leaned toward Nisrine with a lopsided grin. "So… still feeling adventurous?"

Nisrine looked between the two of them. "I'm not trying to start a war. I just want to know the truth. About the worlds. About magic. About my mother."

Dade tilted his head. "That's a tall order. You might have better luck starting a war."

She didn't smile. "Do you know anything about her?"

Dade glanced at Elaila, then back at Nisrine. "We've heard the name, sure. Everyone has. But if you're asking whether we know what happened to her?" He shook his head. "No one does. Not really."

"She didn't vanish," Nisrine said, almost to herself. "People say she vanished. Like she dissolved into legend. But she didn't. She was taken. Or she left… for a reason."

Elaila sat forward slightly. "That may be. But if she left, she covered her tracks so well that no one has ever been able to trace her. That kind of silence? That takes intention."

"Or power," Dade added. "The kind that breaks things just by shifting."

Nisrine's throat tightened. "But she could still be alive."

"Maybe. Or maybe the path she took changed her beyond recognition." Elalia said after a moment.

"You sound like you think she crossed worlds," Nisrine said.

"We don't know what to think," Elaila replied. "Only that she disappeared, and that magic reacted violently around the same time. That's all we have. Rumors. Whispers."

Dade tossed some pine needles into the fire and watched them curl to ash. "Which is more than most ever get. Most just disappear and leave nothing behind."

Nisrine thought of the gate. Of the way her magic had twisted when she passed through. Of the way it still itched beneath her skin like a storm pressing against her ribs. "I need to find it. If she left a path, I have to follow it."

"You don't just *follow* magic," Elaila snapped. "You become part of it. Every step alters you. If you're careless, it'll bind you to the wrong place or break you trying to hold both."

"I can take that risk."

"You say that now," Elaila said darkly. "But if the magic inside you grows too strong, you'll begin to pull the worlds together just by breathing."

Nisrine stilled.

Then Elaila stepped forward, her voice lower now. "That's why you need to *control* it. Learn how to suppress it when you must. How to guide it, not just release it."

"Teach me," Nisrine said urgently. "Help me learn to control it before it controls me."

Elaila stared at her for a long time. Dade sighed and muttered, "Here we go."

Finally, Elaila gave the smallest of nods. "Fine. But not because I believe in whatever quest you think you're on. Because if you lose control, we'll all suffer for it."

Dade leaned back with a grin. "That's the warmest answer I've ever seen her give."

Elaila gave him a look that could've turned stone to dust.

Nisrine exhaled slowly, her shoulders relaxing for the first time since she'd stepped through the gate. There were still a hundred questions, and more danger than answers, but for now, she had something real.

Truth. Fragile, flickering like firelight on a matchstick.

And for the first time since leaving her world behind, Nisrine felt the stirrings of direction, not just movement, but purpose.

Chapter 7

The corridors of the royal palace were colder than usual.

Seren moved through them like a shadow, keeping to the lesser-used passages, his boots whispering against polished stone covered in dust. The torches flickered overhead, casting long, distorted silhouettes along the ancient walls carved with Fae sigils, symbols of protection, loyalty, and balance. But now they felt like hollow promises.

King Lonan's war council had gone late into the night. His voice, strained with fury, had echoed through the halls, demanding strategies and contingencies for bringing Nisrine back from the human world. Not to rescue her, but to retrieve her. Contain her.

And though Seren had stood stone-faced beside the gathered advisors, every word had settled in his chest like heavy stones.

Now, with the moon high and the halls emptying, he slipped toward the western gardens. The guards posted near the gates acknowledged him. He was still trusted. Still expected to serve.

A figure waited by the old archway, the flowering vines around her catching the light in soft silver threads. Olesia.

She straightened as he approached, her braid swaying slightly with the motion. Her sharp eyes flicked to him before she turned and led him deeper into the garden. "You're late."

"The council wouldn't stop talking." He followed her, voice low. "They want to send a retrieval unit through the gate today. Six guards, high magic ranks. They're planning to sedate her, if necessary."

Olesia grimaced. "So, they see her as a liability now. Not our princess."

Seren nodded. "The king's rage is warping into something else. Controlling and dark."

They stopped beneath an ancient willow tree; its branches draped like curtains. Olesia knelt, brushing her hand over a stone slab partially buried beneath the roots. A whisper of light shimmered as the old enchantment recognized her touch, revealing a small stash hidden within the earth: scrolls, a satchel of spell crystals, and a pair of thin-bladed daggers wrapped in cloth.

"They're ready," she said softly. "The ones who still believe in her. They remember what Queen Cherith stood for. They want to help."

On Fallen Wings

"How many?" Seren asked.

"Five so far," Olesia replied. "One healer, two spellcasters, a scout, and an archivist from the old libraries. Quiet, loyal, and fed up with the king's fear politics. More will come once they know you're with us."

Seren looked down at his hands. They still carried the memory of Nisrine's wings. He had failed her when it mattered most.

"She trusted me," he said, his voice barely above a whisper. "And I let her walk into a world she didn't even know."

"She trusted you enough to make that choice in front of you," Olesia said. "You didn't stop her, but you didn't betray her either. That matters."

He exhaled sharply. "It doesn't feel like enough."

Olesia laid a hand on his arm. "Then help her now. Help her *still*. This plan of the king's…it will end badly. If they storm through the gate like invaders, they'll provoke everything Nisrine went to prevent. We need another way."

Seren nodded slowly. "Then we find it."

Together, they bent over the scrolls Olesia had gathered. Maps of ancient ley lines, long-forgotten gate markers, and faded records of Fae who had crossed into the human world generations ago. The information was fragmented, half-erased by time and decree, but they studied each line as if it could save her.

Seren's finger hovered over one of the maps, tracing a jagged path that intersected with multiple symbols drawn in silver ink. "These aren't just ley lines," he murmured. "They converge here… and here. Look at the overlap."

Olesia leaned closer, her brow furrowing. "I thought the gate she used was the only one."

"So did I," Seren said. "But these markings, three convergence points, not one." His voice trailed off as realization settled between them.

"They're hidden," Olesia finished, her eyes wide. "Cloaked by magic, or long buried. She could be anywhere with three gates scattered across their world."

"We'll need a way to track her," Seren said. "Not just the gate she used, but her presence, her magic."

Olesia unrolled a smaller parchment, this one written in the looping, unmistakable hand of Queen Cherith. "We might not need to. Cherith left traces… notes about a 'second tether', a magic she shared with Nisrine in secret. A bond that could resonate even across realms. It might still exist."

Seren's eyes lit with the faintest hope. "If we find that bond, if we follow it…"

"Then we find Nisrine before Lonan's guards do," Olesia finished.

Their eyes met in the shadows, a silent pact forming between them. They would not obey the king. They would not let Nisrine be dragged back in chains. They would find her. And this time, Seren would not let her stand alone.

The courtyard was silent in the early morning, bathed in pale gold light that filtered through the high arches. Birds sang in the distance, their melodies thin and wistful. Beneath the oldest willow in the royal gardens. The grass still shimmered with dew. This had once been Nisrine's favorite place, before the burden of the crown settled over her like dusk. And long before she'd stepped through the ancient gate, leaving everything and everyone behind.

Olesia exhaled, the memory returning.

She had been a child when she was first chosen to serve the princess. Not noble-born, not remarkable in any way. But she had been quick. Quiet. Observant. And she had loved the old stories, especially the ones Queen Cherith told, seated on a moss-covered stone in this very garden, her daughter curled up beside her.

Olesia had watched them from the shadows then, small and shy, until one day, the queen called her forward.

"You listen better than most," Cherith had said, her smile kind. "Perhaps it's time someone listened to you."

That was the beginning.

In time, Olesia had become Nisrine's closest confidante, at least, when Seren wasn't around. But where Seren challenged the princess, drove her to strength, Olesia offered something else. Steadiness. She smoothed the sharp edges, balanced the storm with calm. She knew when to speak and when to remain still. And above all, she knew how to keep secrets.

Now, she moved from the willow toward the shadowed edge of the courtyard, where Seren waited. He stood cloaked in his formal guard uniform.

"You spoke with Captain Aeron?" she asked quietly.

He nodded. "He's with us. And two others from the outer patrol. Quiet loyals. They won't betray us."

"That's ten of us," she murmured.

They fell into step, careful not to attract attention. The hallways, once filled with the casual rhythm of daily life, now thrummed with quiet tension. Guards lined the corridors in pairs instead of singles, their eyes sharper, hands resting closer to the hilts of their weapons. Conversations died the moment they passed. Even the castle's magic, subtle and ever present, felt more watchful, as though the walls themselves had been instructed to listen.

Outside the strategy wing, a set of heavy doors remained shut where they had once stood open. Behind them, the low murmur of voices, strategists, perhaps, or generals, rose and fell like waves against stone. None of those summoned to the war rooms looked directly at Seren or Olesia as they passed, their faces stiff with something close to fear.

Scrolls once stored in archives were now being delivered under guard, vanishing behind sealed doors. Olesia paused as a cloaked courier passed them with a bundle of weathered maps, escorted by a Royal Guard neither of them recognized.

Seren murmured, "He's planning something. Not loud. Not yet. But it's already in motion."

Olesia didn't answer, but her pace quickened.

Olesia's mind raced as she watched another group of soldiers filing through the corridors, quiet, armored, and unmarked. Not palace guards. Hunters. The kind Lonan used when he didn't want to leave a trail.

One of them carried a coil of binding rope etched with dark runes, its glow barely visible beneath the cloth wrap. Another checked a sealed scroll marked with the king's crest, an order, no doubt, already signed.

Her breath caught. He wasn't preparing to welcome Nisrine back. He was preparing to silence her. The realization settled like ice in her chest. This wasn't about rescue. It never had been. To Lonan, everything was a matter of control, of restoring the image of stability, no matter what it cost.

He would retrieve the princess only if it meant restoring order on his terms.

And if that meant stripping her of her voice, her power... even her life?

So be it.

"She won't come back willingly," Olesia said at last.

Seren's jaw flinched. "I know."

They reached the lower wing, where Olesia's quarters lay, tucked behind an unused armory, long forgotten by most of the castle staff. The stone corridor here was quieter, the air colder. No stationed guards. No passing footsteps.

She pressed her hand to the wooden door, a shimmer of runes flared faintly beneath her palm, old magic, concealed and personal. It hissed as it unlocked.

Inside, she lit a single lantern, its flame flickering gently as the wards settled back into the walls. The room was sparse, but layered in subtle protections: woven charms above the windows, ashwood bracing beneath the door, and a polished silver circle etched into the hearthstone.

Not even the king's shadow could reach here easily.

"You've always watched her closer than anyone," Seren said quietly, folding his arms. "Even me."

Olesia didn't respond immediately. Instead, she opened a drawer and retrieved a folded piece of parchment, an old drawing, faded by time. A sketch of a young girl with starlight in her hair, laughing under the willow tree.

"She believed in something none of us did," Olesia said finally. "That the world could be more than this. That magic didn't have to be feared. And just like her mother, the humans might understand us, if only we tried."

"And now she's alone in their world," Seren replied, his voice low. "She shouldn't have gone. I should have stopped her."

"No." Olesia met his gaze. "You couldn't have. And she wouldn't have let you."

Silence settled between them, thick with regret. Then she reached for her belt and drew a thin blade from its sheath, ceremonial, but sharpened with care.

"When the time comes," she said, "we'll go after her. Not with orders from the king. Not with a court mandate. But with love. And with the ones who still believe in her."

Seren studied her for a long moment, then nodded. "We'll need more allies. Quiet ones."

Olesia said, with a small smile. "There are more loyal to her than you think. Some have just forgotten how to hope."

They stood in silence again, but this time, it was purposeful. A calm before the storm. Outside, the wind shifted, carrying with it the scent of rain. Change was coming. And Olesia would face it not as a servant, not as a subject, but as a shield.

For Nisrine. For the memory of Queen Cherith.

And for the future that still flickered like a candle in the dark.

Chapter 8

Nisrine's eyes weren't on Elaila or Dade, they were fixed on the barely visible path that wound its way through the trees, beyond the edge of the camp. Somewhere past the veil of green, nestled in the folds of the land, was the human village.

She had seen flashes of it the day before. Cobblestone streets, the gleam of metal signs, and smoke spiraling from crooked chimneys. Ordinary. Mundane. And yet... utterly magnetic.

"I want to go," she said suddenly.

Elaila didn't look up. "Go where?"

Julie Nelson

"To the village," Nisrine said, stepping closer to the path. "Just for a little while. I want to see it."

Dade glanced up from the blade he was half-heartedly sharpening. "That's a terrible idea. I'm in."

"I'll keep my hood up. I won't talk to anyone. I just," she hesitated, trying to explain the pull inside her chest, "I need to see it. My mother told me stories, but they were always from a distance."

Elaila stood with a sigh, sliding a dagger into her belt with the finality of someone preparing to regret her decisions. "You're not a scholar with a field journal. You're a Fae with unpredictable magic and a glowing target on your back. If they realize what you are, they won't just gossip, they'll try to kill you."

"Then I won't let them see," Nisrine said. "I'll be careful."

Dade tossed his whetstone aside. "Right. Because *careful* is exactly how I'd describe you. Along with 'mysterious royal fugitive' and 'surprisingly persuasive pain in the ass.'"

She tried not to smile.

The wind stirred overhead, brushing leaves into hushed applause. No one spoke for a beat. Then Dade exchanged a long look with Elaila, one of those wordless glances that likely communicated an entire argument.

At last, Elaila gave a clipped nod. "One hour. We go with you. No exceptions."

Nisrine exhaled, relief spreading through her chest. "Thank you."

"Don't thank us yet," Dade muttered as he rose. "Let's just hope no one notices what any of us are."

72

On Fallen Wings

That gave her pause. Nisrine turned. "What do you mean by that?"

Dade shifted his weight, his grin lingering a beat too long before fading. "Oh, you know. The usual. Pointy ears, unnatural elegance, a general aura of 'please interrogate me about my otherworldly heritage.'"

Elaila shot him a warning look sharp enough to skin bark.

Nisrine didn't laugh this time. "No. You're not just talking about me."

A long silence fell. Even the trees seemed to hold their breath. Elaila glared hard at Dade and he suddenly found the grass around his feet very interesting.

"You've felt it," Elaila said, her voice like frost on glass. "The cold that lingers too long when we're near. How we don't eat. Don't sleep. How we don't sit too close to the fire."

Nisrine's heartbeat slowed. She remembered Elaila's eyes catching red in the firelight. Dade vanishing into the shadows like he belonged to them. The way neither of them ever really blinked enough.

"You're…" She swallowed. "You're vampires."

Dade raised a hand. "Guilty. But on the scale of terrifying blood-sucking night monsters, we're, like, a three out of ten. Maybe a six when Elaila hasn't had enough to drink."

Elaila gave him a flat stare. "We've survived because we adapted. We protect the balance. We feed on animals when we must. And occasionally… from humans who offer."

Nisrine frowned. "Offer?"

Elaila crossed her arms, her tone carefully neutral. "There are still humans who believe our kind is something to be

73

worshipped. Admired. They romanticize the old stories. Some of them crave it. See it as intimate, sacred, even beautiful."

Dade smirked. "Some bring gifts. One recited a love letter while I was drinking. I almost blushed."

"I gagged," Elaila muttered, dry as dust. "It was embarrassing for everyone."

Nisrine's brows lifted. "And… you accept?"

"If the intention is clear and the choice is theirs," Elaila said. "Never without consent. That's the only way the balance holds."

Nisrine looked between them, one composed like a blade, the other flippant like a bard with a death wish.

"That's why you're helping me," she said slowly.

Dade nodded. "You're not the only one balancing between two worlds. We've been here for… longer than you can imagine."

Nisrine breathed in deeply, the forest air tinged with pine and damp earth.

They were dangerous, but they hadn't killed her. Hadn't turned her away. That counted for something.

"Okay," she said finally, steadying herself. "Then let's make sure none of us get noticed."

Dade grinned. "Fantastic. A royal fugitive, a reluctant assassin, and a snarky vampire walk into a human village. What could possibly go wrong?"

On Fallen Wings

The road to the village sloped gently downward, flanked by crumbling stone fences and wild rose bushes bursting through the cracks. Nisrine tugged the hood of her borrowed cloak lower, her fingers brushing the edges of the coarse human cloth. The weight of it was unfamiliar, itchy, and dull compared to the silk-dusted glamour of the Fae realm. Beside her, Elaila moved like a wraith: silent, elegant, and completely alert. Dade, as usual, strolled with an exaggerated nonchalance, but even he couldn't mask the sharpness in his eyes.

"You remember the rules?" Elaila asked, her voice low and clipped.

Nisrine nodded. "Don't speak unless spoken to. Stay close."

"And absolutely no drawing attention," Elaila added. "Which you are very, very bad at."

Dade snorted. "Let her breathe, Elaila. If she combusts from stress before we even hit the market, it'll be *your* mess to clean up."

Nisrine didn't respond. Her gaze had already wandered forward, to where the trees broke open into the human settlement. The sight made her stop in her tracks.

The village wasn't large, but it pulsed with life. Smoke curled lazily from thatched chimneys. Bright clothes were strung between windows. Merchants barked prices at haggling buyers while chickens squawked freely between their feet. There was nothing regal or orderly about it. Everything jostled for space and attention, but somehow, it *worked*.

She took a step forward. Then another.

The smells; roasting meat, crushed herbs, iron from the blacksmith's forge, clung to the air sharp and vivid, impossible

75

to ignore. Nisrine felt a strange pang in her chest. There was so much she'd never known to miss.

Dade watched Nisrine take in her first sight of humans and smiled faintly. He stepped to her side and simply said, "Welcome to Laurelglade."

They entered the square without a word. Elaila took the lead, her gaze flicked through the crowd like a blade through tall grass. Dade lingered closer to Nisrine's side, hands in his coat pockets, whistling softly through his teeth.

No one paid them much attention as they entered. Nisrine kept her head down, but her eyes drank in everything. The way the humans greeted each other, the way they bartered over simple goods like salted fish and dyed fabric. It was so different from the quiet reverence of the Fae courts, the stillness of her kingdom's rituals. This world was raw and real.

Nisrine paused by a stall selling glass trinkets. Small, colorful birds with delicately curved wings. Her breath caught. One of them looked exactly like the crystal sparrows that used to sing in her mother's garden. She reached out, brushing her fingers against the glass.

"Beautiful, aren't they?" the shopkeeper said, a round-faced woman with kind eyes and flour-dusted sleeves. "Made by my son. He's got the gift in his hands, he does."

Nisrine forced a smile. "They're lovely."

The woman squinted at her from under bushy brows. "You from the hills? Haven't seen you before."

Elaila stepped in quickly, her tone easy. "Just passing through."

The woman nodded, her expression warming. "Ah. You traveling far?"

On Fallen Wings

"Far enough," Elaila replied with an easy smile. "But the road's been kind so far."

"Glad to hear it," the woman said. "It's rare to meet polite company these days. Safe travels to you."

Nisrine offered a small smile. "Thank you."

They moved on quickly and passed a stall selling old books, their leather bindings curling at the edges. A red-spined volume caught her eye, familiar script, inked with a delicate silver vine pattern that mirrored the Fae archives back home. She stepped forward instinctively, reaching out to trace the spine. The silver vines seemed to gleam brighter in her presence.

"Nisrine," Elaila scolded.

Too late. The bookseller, a stooped man with sharp eyes, looked up.

"Odd fingers you've got," he said. "You a foreigner?"

"I... yes," she stammered, too honest, too quickly.

The man narrowed his eyes.

Dade appeared beside her quickly. "We're passing through," he said smoothly. "Hired her out of Bellwater. Can't read a word, but fascinated by books."

"Huh," the man grunted, unconvinced.

They moved on. Elaila didn't speak, but the look of her anger pressed against Nisrine like a second cloak. Dade fell in beside her and muttered, "Next time, maybe let Elaila hold your leash. Or your hands."

"I didn't mean to," she started.

"I know," he said. "But not meaning to won't keep your head on your shoulders."

Julie Nelson

The market grew thicker with noise. A woman peddling cups sang above the crowd. A boy darted past with a string of beads clutched in his hand, chased by a red-faced vendor. Nisrine felt herself drawn to the chaos, to the unruliness of it all. It was messy. Human. *Alive.*

They paused near a stall filled with tiny clockwork creatures. Metal frogs that jumped when wound, birds that flapped their brass wings with a gentle whir.

"How do they move?" Nisrine asked before she could stop herself.

The man looked up, surprised by her question. He dusted his worn and stained apron with soot-smudged hands. "Gears and wire, miss. A little trick of balance, a little spark of heat. Like magic, some say." He smiled, revealing crooked teeth. "But it's just clever hands and patience."

Nisrine crouched, watching the little frog hop across the tabletop. "Still," she said softly, "there's wonder in it."

The man chuckled. "Aye. Most folk don't notice, but you've got an eye for it."

Elaila cleared her throat behind her, shifting her weight with silent unease. Dade stood just a few steps back, his arms crossed and expression unreadable.

The clockmaker noticed them too. His gaze lingered on Elaila's stillness, the way Dade's eyes moved like a hunter tracking prey. Something flickered in his expression, uncertainty, perhaps, but he said nothing more as Nisrine straightened and offered a quiet thank-you.

They turned down another street, this one lined with wooden homes and open shutters, voices drifting from doorways. A child, mud-streaked and barefoot, ran past and skidded to a stop at the sight of Nisrine. Her eyes went wide, staring openly.

"You're not from here," the girl whispered.

Nisrine smiled gently and whispered back with a smile in her voice. "No. I'm just visiting."

The girl tilted her head. "Your eyes are weird. Pretty, though. Like grass and honey mixed up."

Before Nisrine could respond, a woman's voice called from a nearby porch. "Cecily! Come away from there!" The girl hesitated, then darted off with a giggle. Nisrine stood still for a moment, that strange ache rising again in her chest.

"She wasn't afraid," she said quietly.

"Not all humans are," Dade said, stepping beside her. "Children even less so. They haven't been taught to fear yet."

Elaila frowned. "But they will be. Which is why we don't linger."

By the time they reached the outer square, the air had grown cooler, touched with dusk. A trio of older men sat around a cracked stone fountain, muttering about taxes and wolves in the hills. Two women argued over a bolt of fabric, their laughter bubbling beneath their raised voices. A man sang as he worked at a forge, sweat glistening on his arms. A church bell rang in the distance, hollow and low.

They passed a group of children gathered near a storyteller, an old woman perched on a stool with a circle of rapt faces at her feet. As they passed, Nisrine couldn't help herself. She slowed, listening.

"...and the Fae Queen's wings were glass, so fine and terrible that even a whisper could shatter them," the woman said. "But it was not the Queen you had to fear; it was her daughter. The hidden one. The one they say could command storms."

A chill passed through Nisrine's bones. Her footsteps faltered.

"Keep moving," Elaila hissed under her breath.

But Nisrine didn't. She turned, fully facing the storyteller. Something in her chest... pride? pain?... refused to let her walk away.

"That's not at all right," she said confidently.

Too late, she realized the words had escaped aloud.

The woman stopped mid-sentence. The children turned. A few adults nearby turned as well. And one of them, a tall man leaning against a tavern door, arms crossed, straightened suddenly, his gaze snapping to her like a predator who'd caught a scent.

"Nisrine," Elaila said, grabbing her elbow.

Dade followed his stare and muttered a curse. "Shit. Too late. He saw you."

Elaila was already moving, dragging Nisrine toward the alley behind the tavern.

"He's not a merchant," Dade growled. "Not with that stance or those ears. He's Fae and possibly part of your fathers guard searching for you."

They ducked into the shadows. The light and laughter of the village fell away behind them. Nisrine's pulse thudded in her ears, loud as thunder.

"I didn't mean..."

"You *never* mean to," Elaila snapped, her voice steel. "And it's going to get us all killed."

On Fallen Wings

Dade stepped between them. "Later. Save the fight for when we're not being tailed."

He glanced back toward the street, then snapped, "Move."

They slipped through the alley, past refuse bins and laundry lines, winding a path that led back to the outer woods. Behind them, Nisrine heard boots. Slow, deliberate, tracking.

By the time the trees swallowed them, dusk had become full twilight. Their camp was still distant, but familiar scents, pinesap, moss, wet bark, wrapped around them like a forgotten lullaby.

Only now did Nisrine speak again. "He saw me."

Dade looked over his shoulder, then exhaled through his nose. "No. He saw *someone*. But he'll ask questions. They'll come."

Elaila snapped, "You have to stop thinking this place is a dream, Nisrine. It isn't. It *will* turn on you."

Nisrine nodded. This time, she said nothing back.

The small, hidden camp came into view, a fire still burned low. Dade immediately took to putting it out completely.

Chapter 9

Elaila's face hardened. She cursed and muttered under her breath, her hand instinctively reaching for the dagger at her belt. The swift motion betrayed an urgency Nisrine hadn't seen before. She was no longer the calm, calculated guide. Now, she was a seasoned warrior, fully alert and prepared for battle.

Nisrine's heart pounded harder as the realization set in. Gone was the quiet wonder of exploring a new world.

Elaila's hand gripped the dagger's hilt with a force that could shatter bone, her fingers steady but tinged with fear that she didn't allow to surface. The cool composure she'd maintained up until this point had been replaced by something raw, something primal. The air around her seemed to crackle with a readiness, as though Elaila had shed every trace of pretense and became the blade she held.

A twig snapped in the distance. Sharp. Deliberate.

Not wind. Not animal.

Dade froze beside the dying fire, his nostrils flaring as he tilted his head toward the trees. "They're close," he murmured, voice stripped of humor. "Too close for the head start we got."

Nisrine's breath caught. The scent of smoke still lingered faintly, a trace they couldn't fully erase. She strained to listen, and this time she heard it too. The barely-there rustle of leaves, the whisper of movement just beyond the treeline. Not a charge. A slow, methodical encroachment.

Surrounding.

"They tracked us fast," Elaila said, almost to herself. Her tone was level, but something glinted behind her eyes. A memory, perhaps, of how this always began.

Another sound. A boot brushing against rock. Then silence.

The kind that listens.

"What do we do?" Nisrine demanded, her voice sharp, but beneath the sharpness was an edge of panic she couldn't quite suppress. She felt her heartbeat quicken, her pulse now pounding in her throat.

"We fight," Dade answered, his voice low and strained, tight with tension. "You hide."

His hand never strayed far from the sword at his side, a silent reminder of the violence that was about to erupt. His eyes darted toward the trees surrounding them, scanning the shadows as if he could already sense the danger creeping closer. The humor that usually danced in his gaze was gone, replaced by something cold and dangerous.

The forest, which earlier had felt like a sanctuary, now felt like a prison closing in on her. The trees loomed like silent watchers, and every whisper of wind seemed to carry the scent of danger. Her hands trembled as she clutched at the fabric of her cloak, trying to steady herself, to regain control of a situation that had suddenly spiraled beyond her understanding.

Before anyone could say anything else, the woods around them seemed to come alive. The shadows shifted, a presence materializing from the very heart of the forest. Figures stepped out from the darkness, cloaked in black. The cut of their garments marked them as King Lonan's royal guards, but there was nothing noble in their bearing. Their eyes cast an eerie, predatory glow that made Nisrine's stomach tighten. Their wings were nowhere to be seen. The air felt thick with a foreboding magic that crawled under her skin.

The look in their eyes was unnatural. There was no softness in it, no trace of the beauty that lived in the magic of the Fae. It was the dark, hungry look of something else entirely. Something wicked. Nisrine's breath caught in her throat as the forest around them seemed to shrink, the trees bending closer as if they too sensed the approaching danger.

Their weapons gleamed with magic, but twisted, tainted. It hummed with power, like a living thing waiting to strike. The sharp, metallic scent filled her nose as she could feel the hum of their energy growing stronger, the air now thick with a power she had never felt before. Nisrine's heart raced. She didn't understand it. This wasn't magic like hers. This was something foreign, something alien.

Elaila cursed under her breath again, the word a hiss of defiance, her body tensing as she quickly assessed their position. Her eyes flicked toward Nisrine, then to Dade. "Here we go," she whispered, her voice tight.

As the guards drew closer, surrounding them in a tightening circle, Nisrine's mind raced. This was it. There was no turning back now. The life she had known, the quiet isolation of her world, had been shattered by a single decision. The calm she had grown accustomed to had evaporated, replaced by an ever-tightening noose of fear. Her pulse hammered in her ears as her legs felt unsteady, almost as if the ground itself were shaking beneath her.

She glanced at Dade, who stood with his back to hers, his sword raised in preparation, his eyes darting between the advancing guards. Beside him, Elaila was steady, her eyes flickering between the enemies, waiting for the right moment to strike.

The guards movements were synchronized, fluid and precise, as if they had rehearsed this countless times before. Each movement was calculated, deliberate. Every step they took seemed to bring them closer, tighter, like a noose around her throat. The air was suffocating.

One of the guards, the tallest of the group, took a deliberate step forward. As he raised his head, the hood that had concealed his features slipped back. His skin was rough and weathered, and long black hair, partly tied back, framed the sharp lines of his face. His Fae ears jutted through the strands, unmistakable. His eyes fixated on Nisrine with an unnerving intensity. As cold and unyielding as the steel in his hands.

A slow, mocking grin spread across his face as he sneered, his voice laced with disdain and unspoken triumph. "Hello, Nisrine," he drawled, his voice a purr that dripped with disdain. "Your father has been looking for you."

The words struck her like a blow, but she refused to let them see her cower. She forced herself to meet his gaze.

"You're mistaken," she said, trying to steady her breath, her voice trembling despite her best efforts. "I'm not who you think I am."

The guard's laugh was dark and cruel. It echoed through the clearing, sending a shiver down Nisrine's spine. "You can deny it all you want, Princess," he said, "But you can't hide from your blood. The magic recognizes you."

Dade shifted his stance; his body angled protectively in front of her. His hand tightened around the hilt of his sword, knuckles white. "If you want her, you'll have to go through us," he said, his voice low and dangerous.

Elaila didn't say a word. She simply crouched, shifting her weight as she sized up the enemy. The dagger in her hand gleamed faintly, the edge sharp enough to cut through the silence itself.

Chapter 10

Nisrine's heart hammered in her chest and in her ears. *The magic recognizes me?* If they knew who she was, they would stop at nothing to take her. Or worse, destroy her. The realization sent a cold wave of fear through her, but there was no time to dwell on it.

"We're not here for a conversation," another guard said, his voice cold as steel. His hood obscured most of his face, but the smirk in his tone was unmistakable. He held a long, curved blade, its edges glowing with a sickly blue light. "Give yourself up. It'll be easier for all of us." His words were casual, almost bored, but the way he stood, ready to strike, his fingers twitching on the handle of his weapon, told a different story.

There was no real offer of mercy here. Only control. Only power.

Nisrine clenched her fists, a strange energy surging within her, something raw and ancient. She took a step back, glancing at Elaila, who stood rigid beside her.

"They won't stop," Elaila muttered, her voice barely audible. "Not unless we force them to."

The guards moved as one, their formation tightening, step by step, their footsteps eerily silent against the forest floor. Nisrine could hear the faint rustle of leather and cloth, the click of a blade unsheathing, the hum of magic crackling in the air like static before a storm.

Her mind spun. What could she do? What chance did she have against enemies who had spent years preparing for this exact moment?

Then, a voice, soft yet firm, whispered in the safety of the palace gardens.

"This word is older than time, Nisrine. If you ever need it, let it guide you." Her mother's voice.

There was one advantage she had: her magic. Even without her wings, she could feel the pulse of it within her, as steady and strong as her heartbeat. She closed her eyes for the briefest moment, reaching for the only weapon she truly had.

An ancient word formed on her lips. A whisper of power passed down through her bloodline, a spell her mother had once murmured in secret. The syllables felt foreign yet familiar, like a melody she had always known.

"Shaelthar."

The moment the word left her lips, a brilliant burst of light erupted from her, illuminating the camp like a midday sun.

The guards recoiled, staggering back with startled cries as the force of it blasted outward. They shielded their faces with their arms. Some even thumped their swords against the one next to them.

"Run!" Elaila's voice cut through the chaos like a whip. Nisrine didn't hesitate. She turned and sprinted into the trees, her heart pounding in rhythm with her frantic footsteps. The forest blurred around her, streaks of moonlight flickering between the branches. *Faster. Faster.* She missed her wings, gods, how she missed them, but she couldn't stop.

Behind her, the guards recovered fast. She could hear their pursuit, their footfalls sharp against the undergrowth. A sharp crackle of energy surged through the air. Magic. Nisrine barely had time to swerve as a projectile, bright and seething with unnatural energy, shot past her shoulder, exploding against a tree in a burst of blue fire. The wood groaned as the bark splintered and exploded outward in a shower of embers. The scent of scorched wood filled the air.

She zigzagged through the trees, weaving through the thick undergrowth, her heart thundering. She could hear them behind her.

Nisrine ran, but the sounds of battle behind her made it impossible to ignore what she was leaving behind. The clash of steel, the crackling energy of magic colliding, the sharp grunts of exertion. All of it filled the air in a violent symphony.

Elaila had stayed behind.

Through the dim light, Elaila was moving like a shadow, her twin daggers glistening with fresh blood. One of the guards lunged at her, swinging a wickedly curved blade meant to incapacitate, not kill. Elaila dodged effortlessly, twisting her body to avoid the strike before countering with a swift slash across his arm.

The guard let out a snarl of pain, "You fight like a cornered beast," he spat, gripping his wounded arm. "But you're outnumbered."

Elaila smirked, flicking the blood from her dagger. "But you're *outclassed*."

The guard's eyes widened. Before the guard could react, she was already moving. She ducked low, sweeping his legs out from under him. He hit the ground hard, but he recovered quickly, rolling to his feet and hurling a bolt of crackling blue magic toward her. Elaila barely had time to dodge as the energy seared past her, scorching the bark of a nearby tree.

The guard advanced again, striking fast. He was stronger than she'd anticipated. His attacks were relentless, precise. She blocked his next blow with the flat of her dagger, but the force sent a jolt through her arm. He was trying to wear her down, to break her defenses.

Elaila gritted her teeth. *Fine. Let's see how well you fight when you're off-balance.*

She feinted left, drawing him into overextending his next strike. The moment his footing faltered, she twisted, using his own momentum against him. In a blur of motion, she drove her dagger into his side, the blade sinking deep between his ribs.

The guard gasped, eyes wide with shock, but Elaila didn't give him time to react. She yanked the blade free and spun, delivering a swift kick to his chest that sent him sprawling. He hit the ground with a thud, clutching his wound.

She didn't wait to see if he would get back up. More were coming. She could hear them. Footsteps in the underbrush, voices barking orders. They were closing in fast.

Breathing hard, Elaila turned her gaze toward the trees, toward where Nisrine had disappeared into the forest. She had to hope she had made it.

With one last glance at the fallen guard, Elaila tightened her grip on her weapons and sprinted into the darkness.

Nisrine kept running. Panic surged. She needed to fight back. *Do something!* As if in answer, her hands tingled, then burned. She gasped as light flickered around her fingers, a glowing aura forming, wild and untamed.

The forest pulsed around her, *with her,* its magic waking in response to her fear. It recognized her, just as the guard had said. The power swelled in her palms, then shot outward in a blinding arc, striking the nearest one square in the chest.

He let out a strangled cry before collapsing, the light swallowing him whole.

The other guards hesitated, visibly shaken. They had expected a frightened girl. An easy target. Not this.

Then a voice cried out. "Look out!"

Dade's voice. Urgent. Desperate.

A rough hand appeared suddenly from behind her, gripping her wrist with a bruising force. Fingers like iron clamped around her arm, yanking her off balance. She gasped, twisting as she fell, hitting the ground hard. Pain flared through her side. The guard's expression twisted with triumph. "Got you now!"

Before Nisrine could react, another form crashed into them. Dade.

The impact sent them all sprawling, Dade's sword clattering as he wrestled with the guard. The two of them grappled, rolling over dirt and leaves, each fighting for dominance.

Nisrine scrambled to her feet, her hands still glowing with raw power. "Dade…" Her voice was torn between relief and fear.

He twisted, locking eyes with her even as he still wrestled with the guard, his tone sarcastic and dry even in the chaos. "Really? This is the thanks I get?"

She hesitated. Her heart screamed at her to stay, to fight with him. But there was no time.

"Thank you," she whispered, her voice barely a breath.

Dade gritted his teeth. "Just go already! I can't keep this bastard down much longer!"

Nisrine turned and ran. She didn't look where she was going. She just ran.

Then, a pulse.

The air shifted with a thrum of ancient magic brushing against her skin like static.

Too close. Too fast.

On Fallen Wings

Before she could stop herself, the magic caught her. She had run toward the gate without realizing it.

And in a heartbeat, she was gone.

The last thing she heard was Dade's shout, lost in the wind. Then, silence.

The trees, the guards, the battle, all blurred into nothingness.

Chapter 11

The world dissolved into a dizzying vortex of light and shadow. For a moment, she felt like she was being torn apart, her body flickering between realities, pulled by forces she couldn't fully comprehend.

Then, with a jarring lurch, the world snapped back into place.

She tumbled out of the gate and landed on solid ground with a soft thud. Her heart pounded in her chest, and her breath came in quick, shallow gasps. She had made it. She had escaped.

But this…

This wasn't her Fae realm she had come from.

Nisrine scrambled upright, her eyes scanning the unfamiliar landscape. The energy in the air felt different. Older somehow. Still the human world, but not the same part of it. Wherever she had landed, it wasn't near Dade or Elaila.

Her stomach dropped.

The gate had brought her somewhere else.

Her brow furrowed as she tried to make sense of it. Was that even possible? She had only known of one gate. One crossing point between the Fae realm and the human world. Had the magic shifted? Or... was there more than one?

Nisrine took a tentative step forward. She couldn't afford to stay still. Not with Lonan's guards wherever they were, looking for her now. She had no idea where the gate had brought her, but she couldn't stay here. She needed to find shelter, a place to hide.

The trees here weren't like the ones in the Fae realms. They were rougher, their bark mottled, their branches gnarled into unnatural shapes. This place was unlike anything she had ever seen before. She took a step forward, then another, careful not to disturb the quiet more than necessary.

A deep stillness settled around her. No birdsong. No insects. Not even the rustle of a breeze.

She pressed a hand against a tree, trying to feel for any lingering pulse of life. But there was only silence. This forest was not alive the way hers had been. It tolerated her. Watched her.

"Where am I?" she whispered aloud, her voice barely audible over the sound of her own breathing.

She walked for what felt like hours, her body sore from the rough landing, her feet damp with dew and dirt. The path she followed was barely visible, more suggestion than trail, broken only by the occasional stone or twisted root that jutted up through the moss.

Memories flickered through her mind like fragile feathers on the wind. Her father's warning. Seren's pleading voice. Her wings, left behind. A phantom pain tingled across her shoulder blades, sharp and sudden. She ground her teeth and kept walking.

Eventually, she stumbled across a stream. A narrow ribbon of water, clear but slow. She knelt beside it, cupping her hands and drinking deeply, the cold biting at her throat. When she looked, her reflection stared back at her from the surface. Mud-smeared cheeks, wind-tangled hair clinging to her face, a scrape along her chin where a branch, or a blade, had caught her. But it wasn't just the dirt or bruises that made her pause.

Her skin shimmered faintly. Not from the light but from something deeper. Magic clung to her skin faint and flickering. For a breath, her reflection shifted and rippled with an echo of wings she no longer possessed.

Gone was the softness that had once marked her. In its place was a tension behind her gaze, a weight she hadn't noticed carrying until now.

"I'm not the same," she murmured, watching the image blur and reform. "Not anymore."

A sound snapped through the trees behind her. She whirled, heart hammering. Nothing. Only the forest, holding its breath.

Then another sound. Closer this time. A shuffle, a crunch, a flicker of movement in her peripheral vision.

She stood slowly, brushing her damp hands against her cloak. "If someone's there... I'm not looking for a fight."

No answer.

She turned in a slow circle, straining her senses. The silence had shifted. It wasn't empty anymore. It was expectant. Something was watching her.

"Hello?" she called into the trees, louder this time.

Still nothing.

She moved on, this time slower, more deliberate, testing the forest's response with each footfall. The path began to rise, and soon she found herself climbing a ridge. She was breathing harder now, her limbs aching, but the need to find shelter drove her forward.

And then she stepped into a clearing. Stones, half-buried in the dirt, arranged in a pattern too deliberate to be natural. A ring. Old. Forgotten. Choked with moss and lichen.

Nisrine stepped inside the circle, drawn by instinct.

She felt it immediately. Not a sound or a vision, just a shift in the air, like walking through a curtain of memory. Her skin prickled. The magic here was faint but familiar, like an echo of something she once knew. Her heart beat faster. She had no name for this place, but it felt... significant.

She closed her eyes, letting herself breathe in the silence.

But instead of darkness behind her lids, there was red. Vivid, like sunlight through blood. It wasn't painful, but it was wrong.

And in that strange, brilliant stillness, something stirred within her.

Her mother's voice. A whisper. A memory she hadn't heard in years.

"The oldest places remember us, even when we forget ourselves."

Nisrine dropped to one knee, placing a palm to the earth inside the stone ring. A pulse. Weak, but there. A remnant of the old world, something from before the divide.

She wasn't sure how long she knelt there before another sound pulled her back. A very human footstep on brittle leaves.

She rose, slowly, turning toward the source. A figure stepped from the trees. At first, Nisrine tensed, but the figure didn't seem hostile. In fact, it looked... almost familiar. A tall man, dressed in dark, weathered clothes, his face partially hidden by the hood of his cloak. But there was something in his posture, in the way he moved. Like he was waiting for her.

"You look lost." he said, his voice deep and oddly calm.

Nisrine froze.

"Maybe I am." she said, her voice sharp, her eyes narrowing. She instinctively reached for the magic within her, just in case she needed to defend herself.

The man's lips quirked into a small, knowing smile. "You came through the gate, didn't you?"

She dusted her hands off. "How did you know that?"

"Because that place hasn't stirred in years. And now it hums like it's waking up."

"I'm Nisrine," she said cautiously.

The man tilted his head slightly. Then, without a word, he stepped forward and lowered his hood.

Nisrine's breath caught.

He was young, no older than she, perhaps, but his eyes were ancient, filled with a depth that seemed to pierce through her, as though he had seen things no one should ever witness. His dark brown hair fell in waves around his face, his grey colored eyes were the most beautiful grey she had ever seen, and the faintest trace of something, some kind of magic, seemed to pulse around him, like a low hum in the air. She then stared at his ears. They weren't exactly as pointed as her own but they were very close.

Nisrine then added, "I am the Princess of the Kingdom of Constalatia. But I'm not here on royal business. I'm here because I need answers."

He hesitated. Then said, "You've felt it, haven't you? The magic within you calls to this world. But you don't know how to control it. Not yet. And that's why I'm here."

Nisrine frowned, her pulse quickening. "*Why* are you here? Who are you?"

The man stepped closer, his steps light but deliberate, the faint crackle of dried leaves under his boots. His eyes softened, though there was a sadness in them, like a shadow he had carried for too long. "My name is Corvan," he said at last, his voice a low murmur that seemed to resonate with the forest itself. "I'm… I'm one of the last human-Fae hybrid descendants who remembers the old magic. The magic that once bridged our worlds."

Nisrine blinked at him, stunned. *A hybrid?* She had heard stories of such beings long ago but never seen one. Most believed they had died out, faded into myth with the ruin of the old world.

"I didn't even know there were any of your kind left," she said softly, her voice trembling with wonder and an undercurrent of dread.

Corvan's expression shifted, something between sorrow and resignation. "You weren't meant to. Most have been forgotten. The rest were erased." He met her gaze then, unflinching. "You've been raised with fragments, Princess. In a kingdom wrapped in beauty... and illusion. But the truth is darker than you can even imagine."

She held his gaze. The way he said *Princess,* not with reverence, but with a twinge of disdain, made her chest tighten as though he had cut her with it.

Corvan stepped closer, voice low. "You were protected, yes, but you were also kept blind. The forest you knew, the rituals, the silence of your court... they were meant to shield you from what came before. And now here you are, standing on the edge of something no one has dared touch since before you were born. Standing where you shouldn't be."

Something in her snapped, some defiance that had always simmered in her blood. She took a sharp step toward him, leaving the circle of stones, fists clenched at her sides. "I didn't come all this way to be told to turn back. I gave up *everything* to come through that gate. My wings, my court, my place in that gilded cage, gone. So, tell me. Tell me everything."

But even as the words left her, her vision blurred. The trees around them seemed to ripple, the sky above them yawning too wide, too endless. Her thoughts spun in tight circles. Fragments of her mother's warnings, the ache in her father's voice, Seren's haunted silence, the pulse of magic inside of her that she couldn't yet control.

Her hand flew to her forehead, pressing hard against her temples.

Corvan's eyes sharpened with concern. "Nisrine?"

She met his gaze, her voice barely audible. "I… I think I need to rest."

Her strength buckled beneath the storm in her mind. Her knees gave out, her body folding as darkness closed in.

Corvan caught her, his arms steady around her. She felt his calloused fingers gently sweep the hair from her face. A simple touch, grounding, and strange. The world dimmed at the edges, her thoughts unspooled into nothingness. She let herself lean into him, her last breath a whisper of exhaustion. Then everything went black.

Chapter 12

The moment she fell, Corvan moved without thought.

His arms caught her just before she hit the ground, the sudden stillness of her limp body stirring something deep inside him. She wasn't heavy, not in the physical sense, but the gravity of what she carried pressed down on him all the same. Power radiated from her, even unconscious, a whisper of old magic curling through the air like smoke.

He shifted her gently, brushing the hair from her face. Her skin was pale beneath the moonlight, but it glowed faintly, unnaturally. Too much had happened too quickly. He should've warned her. Should've eased her in. Now here she was, this real being from the world of stories told in whispers by the humans, fallen into his arms like a dropped star.

And stars were dangerous things.

Corvan exhaled slowly and rose with her in his arms. He didn't head toward his home. Not yet.

Instead, he took her to the small cave he'd prepared two days ago, when he first felt the gate stir. A shallow overhang tucked beneath a curtain of roots and stones. Hidden enough to stay out of sight, open enough to leave in a hurry. It wasn't much. But it wasn't *his* place either. That was the point.

He hadn't planned on bringing anyone anywhere near the life he'd built. This was temporary. Just a place to keep her safe while he figured out what to do next.

He laid her down on a bed of moss and fur-lined cloth, brushing the dirt from her cloak. Then he sat beside her, knees drawn up, hands wrapped around his elbows as the fire in his mind refused to still.

Nisrine.

He had known her name before she ever stepped through the gate. Not because of any royal decree or prophecy, but because of the whispers in the old magic. The ancient thrum in the earth had sung her name for years, *Nisrine, the wild thorned rose. Nisrine, daughter of storm and rain.*

She was a story made flesh, one he'd grown up hearing only in fragments: the last of the royal line untouched by corruption, the child whose mother vanished and whose father ruled through fear disguised as peace. A Fae born too late to change the world, and too early to be forgotten.

And now she was here. In his world. In his care.

Corvan ran a hand through his dark hair, nose scrunching. He had to be careful. The old magic in her would awaken fully now that she was on this side of the gate. And if she wasn't ready…

He glanced at her again.

She looked nothing like the Fae royalty from stories. There was no silver crown on her brow, no cold fire in her expression. Just a curious female who had risked everything to find answers. But beneath the quiet strength in her features, he saw what she bore, the grief, the determination. The sheer force of will that made her step through a gate that hadn't opened in decades.

He should fear her. He should want nothing more than to see her turn back. But he didn't. What he feared was what she might become without the truth. Because Corvan knew better than most what power without understanding could do.

He was five the first time he saw someone die from magic.

His mother's hands had trembled as she pulled him away from the fire, where his best friend lay crumpled. His body scorched from the inside out. Too much magic, too fast. The boy had thought he could control it, bend it to his will. But hybrid blood wasn't made to bear that kind of power. Not without training. Not without sacrifice.

Corvan never forgot.

Even as a child, the magic whispered to him. It hummed in the stones beneath his feet, curled in the wind at his back, and thrummed in his bones on moonless nights. It called to him. Not with words, but with presence. With knowing.

On Fallen Wings

And when he grew old enough to choose for himself, he stopped running from it. Instead, he learned.

He wandered the forgotten ruins where the veil between worlds still felt thin. He collected the scraps of lost lore, piecing together fragments of what the world used to be. He listened to the trees, the wind, and the stones when they whispered the truth about what the Fae were before the barrier. About what they lost. About why the humans turned on them. Not only from fear, but from desperation.

Because magic, once loosed, could not be reclaimed.

Even now, as he sat beside the unconscious Fae princess, those memories rippled through him. Unbidden, insistent.

Nisrine lay still, her breathing slow but steady. Her presence here changed everything. He'd spent years preparing for this moment, for the gate to open again. But now that she was here, flesh and blood and full of volatile power, he realized just how much she didn't know. How much had been kept from her.

Corvan's hands tightened around the hilt of the dagger resting in his lap. It was an old thing, etched with runes long forgotten by most. His mother had given it to him before she died, saying it once belonged to his father, Calreth. He was a Fae warrior. Or maybe a renegade. She'd never been clear.

His mother. She had been the only one who truly saw both sides. The only one who believed peace between their worlds wasn't just a relic of the past. In the quiet hours before dawn, she used to tell him stories of the old days, when humans and Fae lived not just beside each other, but together. Trading knowledge. Sharing harvests. Blending bloodlines.

But those days were long gone now.

Julie Nelson

Corvan's very existence was proof of that broken world. Born of two bloods, but accepted by neither. Humans regarded him with suspicion. Too strange, too quiet, eyes that saw too much. The Fae, those few who still wandered beyond the gate in secret, looked at him like he was a mistake. An echo of something that never should have existed.

Still, his mother had believed in something greater. She said the worlds would reunite someday. That her son, half of one world, half of the other, might be the key to that reconciliation. A bridge.

What began as duty had become a quiet burden, one that settled deeper into his bones with time. And still, he chose to bear it.

Corvan turned his gaze to Nisrine again. She looked younger now. Her presence was Fae, unmistakably so. But there was something in her. Something uncertain, something searching that reminded him of himself.

He should keep his distance. Should leave her here just long enough for her to recover. Long enough to figure out what she was going to do next. That had been the plan.

But the plan hadn't accounted for her collapsing into his arms. It hadn't accounted for the way her magic made the forest *listen*.

He leaned back against the bundle of furs behind him, listening to the wind thread through the branches. It was different. Quieter, older. The magic in her had stirred something ancient, and that awakening would not go unnoticed.

They would come for her. Those who feared what she could become. Humans. Fae. Others.

She was more than just a symbol. She was a female. One who had left everything behind: her crown, her home, her wings, for the chance to find the truth. He owed her that much.

Corvan stiffened.

He couldn't pretend she wasn't already part of this now. He couldn't pretend she wasn't part of *him*.

But telling her the truth wouldn't be easy. It would unravel everything she believed about her people, her parents, and her magic. She had been raised in a palace of beauty, but it was a cage all the same. One wrapped in silk and stories that bent the truth to suit a broken peace.

And now, the burden of that truth fell on him.

With a quiet breath and steady resolve, Corvan bent down and lifted her gently into his arms. She didn't stir. He held her close, the cloak still wrapped around her, and started toward the narrow path that led deeper into the woods.

To his home.

Chapter 13

The morning light spilled softly through the cracks in the weathered walls of the cabin, casting a faint, golden glow across the rough-hewn wood. The air was cool, thick with the scent of clay and the lingering fragrance of wildflowers that grew in the clearing just beyond the doorway. Outside, the rhythmic chirping of distant birds and the faint rustling of the trees blended together in a gentle, peaceful symphony.

Inside, Nisrine stirred beneath a pile of fur blankets, her delicate Fae form nestled in the cozy nook of a raised wooden platform. The fire, still smoldering in the stone hearth, cast flickering shadows that danced on the walls. The faint scent of cedarwood and burning pine mingled with the air around the unfamiliar yet strangely comforting surroundings.

Her hair, still tangled from sleep, shimmered faintly in the dim light, and the ethereal glow of her Fae presence hummed gently beneath her skin. The room was small, humble, but functional. Woven baskets, hand-carved wooden shelves, and a few simple but well-loved tools were scattered around. A small table held a pitcher of water and a mismatched mug, the kind that speaks of a life lived with practicality over luxury.

There was a deep stillness in the room, broken only by the sound of Nisrine's breath as she woke. She sat up, her eyes still heavy from sleep, and took in the sight of Corvan's simple abode. Her mind raced. Memories of her sudden arrival here flooded back. She had left her world, a realm of magic and mischief, to this strange place, a battle with the guards, leaving her new friends, and ended up in the wilds of Corvan's home. The Fae princess, so accustomed to the shimmer of her kingdom's light, was now surrounded by the quiet, raw beauty of the human world.

As she stretched, her fingertips grazed the rough wooden beams above her, grounding herself in this foreign place. The space was simple, but there was a quiet magic in the air here, a sort of pulse that she couldn't quite explain. The cabin, for all its simplicity, felt like a sanctuary. The sound of Corvan's footsteps outside reminded her that she was not alone in this place, but the question lingered: what will she find here, in this world, with a human-fae hybrid whose life seems so starkly different from her own?

As Nisrine stepped lightly from the platform, her bare feet grazed the cool wooden floor, and the world outside seemed to beckon her. The soft rustle of leaves and the distant sounds of nature felt soothing, but there was uncertainty in her heart. Yet, there was something here. A calm she hadn't known before, something in the air that stirred her curiosity.

She moved toward the small window, looking out at the forest beyond. The trees stretched high, their branches swayed in the morning breeze, their leaves a vivid tapestry of greens and golds. It was a scene of tranquil beauty, but still, the echoes of all that had changed in this world and hers lingered.

She heard the steady rhythm of footsteps, the unmistakable sound of Corvan approaching. Her pulse quickened. She hadn't fully processed how she felt about him, about the half-human who took her in without question.

As the door creaked open, Corvan stepped in, his figure filling the entrance with a quiet strength. His dark hair was tousled. His simple tunic of earth-toned cloth marked him as someone who belonged to the land. His eyes met hers, and for a moment, there was an unspoken understanding. He didn't need to say anything. He simply watched her, waiting.

"Good morning," Corvan finally said, his voice warm but cautious. "I thought you might want some breakfast. There's porridge and fresh berries if you're hungry."

Nisrine hesitated. The simple offer seemed almost absurd, too mundane for someone like her, a princess of a realm filled with wonders beyond comprehension. Yet, there was something undeniably comforting in the gesture. She nodded, her voice soft as she replied, "Thank you."

Corvan stepped aside, making way for her to pass. The simple meal that waited on the wooden table seemed so small, but to Nisrine, it felt like an indulgence. As she sat down, she noticed the quiet attention in Corvan's gaze, the way his eyes flickered with curiosity and concern. But also, something else, an earnestness she hadn't encountered in her world.

Before she could say anything, he asked, almost hesitantly, "How do you feel? About being here? Away from your realm?"

Nisrine paused, spoon halfway to her lips. The question lingered in the air, and her heart twisted with thought. Her world is so far away, its light and joy now a distant memory. She wondered if she'd ever return. Or if she even wanted to. She placed the spoon down; her fingers traced the rim of the bowl as she gathered her thoughts.

"I don't know yet," she says quietly, her eyes meeting his. "This place... It's strange. I've never been this far from home before."

Corvan nodded, understanding without needing more explanation. "It must be hard," he said, and there was a flicker of something like sympathy in his eyes. "But you're safe here. I'll protect you. You don't need to worry about anything."

Nisrine felt a strange warmth bloom in her chest at his words. His voice was sincere, and for a fleeting moment, the fear melted away.

She allowed herself to relax, taking a bite of the porridge. The food was simple, but it tasted like comfort. As they ate in companionable silence, the tension that had hung between them began to dissipate, replaced by something new. An unspoken understanding that their worlds were colliding in a way neither of them could fully predict.

And though Nisrine had no idea what the future held, she knew one thing: for now, she had found something she had wanted since her time as a small child with her mother. A Fae ally in this strange human world.

Later Corvan helped Nisrine try a grounding ritual, and she fell over.

Corvan didn't laugh. But only barely.

"You said to feel the roots," she muttered, brushing pine needles from her knees.

"I said to imagine your energy extending downward. I didn't say to physically grow roots," he replied, arms crossed as he leaned against the mossy trunk of a tree. His eyes glinted, amused.

Nisrine narrowed her gaze and turned away, settling once more into her stance. She inhaled and reached inward, calling to the magic beneath her skin. It answered, as always, too fast, too much. The wind stirred sharply around her. Leaves lifted. A shimmer passed through the grass.

And then, the boulder beside her cracked clean down the middle.

Corvan straightened instantly. "Stop. Breathe."

She did. The magic stilled, reluctantly.

Silence fell.

"I didn't *mean* to," she said quietly.

"I know." Corvan stepped into the circle of flattened grass beside her. "That's the point. You're not *commanding* it.

You're *feeling* it. It's like a river. Don't build a dam, just... learn when to dip your hands in."

Nisrine nodded, frowning in concentration.

Their training took them through meadows where old glyphs lay buried under layers of lichen, through pockets of the forest where the air grew too still and the animals kept far away. In each place, Corvan guided her, not like a tutor, but like a translator. Helping her understand a language her blood already knew but her heart did not.

Sometimes she succeeded. Once, she coaxed a dying sapling to bloom.

Sometimes she did not. Once, she melted a hole in the ground.

But always, Corvan watched with quiet intensity.

And between the rituals, there were walks.

He pointed out small things. The way humans marked time with bells in the distant village. How they planted by moon cycles. How they left offerings of stones or bread at shrines.

Nisrine asked questions that caught him off guard. "Why do they fear the woods? So you just... give this shiny circle to someone, and they hand you food?"

One evening, as the fire crackled low and the stars crowded close overhead, Nisrine sat cross-legged in the grass with her palms against the earth. Her eyes were closed, lips moving with some half-formed chant Corvan had taught her earlier. She didn't see him watching her. How her hair stirred with the wind, how her fingers glowed faintly at the tips. How she exhaled with reverence, as if listening to a voice buried deep inside the land.

When she opened her eyes, he was already turning away.

By the third morning, she was laughing at his dry remarks. By the fourth, she was matching his pace through the woods with ease. By the fifth, he found himself waiting for her questions, for the way she tilted her head when something confused her. Not just because of the legacy she carried. But because of *her*. Her fierce compassion. Her fire-wrought hope. The way she looked at him like he wasn't broken by what he was, like he wasn't just the byproduct of two warring legacies.

He'd spent his whole life straddling a line between two worlds that didn't want him. But with Nisrine... he didn't feel like a mistake. He felt seen.

And slowly, something within him began to shift.

He had thought his role was to guide her. To keep her from tearing open the past. But with every lesson, every conversation that danced past midnight beneath the stars, he realized something else.

This wasn't just her journey.

It was his, too. A path to reclaim not only the truth, but maybe, for the first time, a place to belong.

The first time Nisrine tried to draw a binding circle, it exploded.

Not dramatically. No flames or thundercaps. But the circle she etched into the ground fizzled out in a puff of white smoke, scattering the crushed herbs she'd carefully placed along its edges and blowing her hair into her eyes.

Corvan coughed and waved the smoke away. "Well, it was *almost* a circle."

Nisrine groaned and tossed the stick of chalk aside. "It *was* a circle. The magic just didn't like it."

"No. *You* didn't like it," Corvan replied evenly. "You're forcing it. Magic doesn't respond well to impatience."

She glared at him, wiping her sooty hands on her cloak. "What am I even binding? The air?" she said, flapping her hands around.

"In this case, yes." He raised an eyebrow in amusement. "A binding circle is about containment. Think of it like a net. If woven correctly, it can hold energy. Or beings. Or even memories." He crouched beside her and tapped the uneven arc she'd drawn in the dirt. "But if the threads are tangled, it unravels."

She frowned. "And if the threads are too tight?"

"Then it snaps back on you."

Nisrine learned that the hard way the next afternoon.

Her second attempt, made with steady lines and whispered syllables held together for five full seconds before a thin whip of magic lashed outward and slapped her palm like a reprimanding teacher.

"Ow!" She shook her hand, scowling at the faint scorch mark.

Corvan, to his credit, didn't smirk. "You're binding too tightly. The circle needs to breathe."

"Circles don't breathe," she muttered, though she knew he was right.

It wasn't until the fifth attempt that something clicked.

They had moved indoors by then. Into Corvan's cabin, warm with firelight and smelling faintly of pine ash and lavender smoke. The floor was swept clean, and she'd taken her time laying the elements in a measured ring: crushed sage at the north, a drop of water from the nearby stream at the south, a sliver of obsidian at the west, and a small feather at the east.

"Let the magic pass through you," Corvan said from behind her. "Don't grab it. Invite it."

She closed her eyes and exhaled. This time, instead of reaching for the power like a weapon, she let it rise slowly, like steam rising from a heated stone. She whispered the words, fingers steady, drawing the final line with care.

"Serathil. Mirelen."

The circle pulsed, once. Then held.

A soft shimmer passed through the air inside the ring, the contained energy flickered like heat haze.
Nisrine blinked. "It worked."

"You did it." Corvan's voice was calm, but his pride was obvious.

Hours later the fire crackled low between them, casting soft orange light against the rough-hewn walls of Corvan's cabin. Outside, the wind stirred the trees in long, sighing breaths, but inside, all was still. Nisrine sat cross-legged on a woven mat, her hair loose around her shoulders, catching the glow of the flames like silk spun from starlight.

They had lapsed into a thoughtful quiet. It was Nisrine who broke the silence.

"Do you remember your father?" she asked, her voice soft. She picked up the basket of berries she had gathered earlier. She ate three at once.

Corvan didn't answer immediately. He reached for a stick and stirred the coals, watching them shift and pulse with heat. "No. Only stories," he said at last. "And shadows."

Nisrine tilted her head. "Was he Fae?" She ate a few more berries.

He nodded. "My mother said he came from the deep woods. One of the last true-blooded ones still wandering. She said he spoke in riddles and touched the earth like it spoke to him. But he didn't stay."

"I'm sorry." She ate more berries.

Corvan gave a small shrug, though his eyes remained fixed on the fire. "He gave her a son. Maybe that's all he was good for. Or maybe he meant to return and never could. I used to wonder. Sometimes I still do."

Nisrine drew her knees to her chest, eating more. "You said you've always felt the magic calling?"

"Yes." He looked up at her. "It's different for me, though. I don't have the same... harmony with it that you do. The Fae side of me wants to flow with it. But the human side..." He tapped his chest lightly. "It wants to contain it. To survive it."

She was quiet for a long moment before speaking again. "Do you ever wish you were just one or the other?"

Corvan blinked at her. The question was so direct. So gently spoken. And yet it struck deeper than he expected. "I used to. All the time. When I was younger, I thought being half of two things meant I was *less* of both. That no matter what I did, I'd never belong."

"And now?"

117

His gaze found hers across the fire, steady and sure. "Now I think it might mean I understand both sides better than anyone. Maybe even better than they understand themselves. That's a kind of power, too."

Nisrine nodded slowly, absorbing his words. "I'm glad you're the one who found me."

Corvan's chest tightened at that. The fire popped, as if in agreement, and the silence between them warmed with something unspoken.

"I think," he said, voice low, "I was always meant to."

She extended the basket of berries to him.

He paused, frowning at the berries she held out so trustingly. "Where did you find these?" he asked, a note of caution in his tone.

"Near the river," she said, shrugging. "They looked… safe enough." She smiled broadly, cheeks flushed from the fire's glow and perhaps from the sweet taste of the berries themselves.

Corvan took the basket from her hands, studying the small fruits carefully. The berries were small and deep violet, their skins glossy and almost wet-looking. A heady, sweet scent rose up, rich but with an undertone of something darker.

He inhaled, brows knitting. "These aren't for eating," he said softly, glancing up to meet her gaze. "Not if you want to stay in the world we're sitting in."

Her smile faltered, and she blinked, suddenly unsteady. She looked at the half-eaten handful in her palm, her fingertips stained with their juice, purple so deep it was almost black. She lifted her fingers to her lips again, slow and dazed. "What… do you mean?"

"They're called Thistlewine Berries," he said, voice even. "Sweet at first. Then they peel your mind back like a flower."

Nisrine's eyes widened, her pupils already dilating as the first hints of the berries taking hold. A slow, almost amused smile curved her lips, "Well," she said faintly, "I suppose I've already begun."

Corvan's eyes showed the flicker of alarm breaking through his composure. He reached out, his fingers brushing her wrist. "You'll be seeing things. Hearing voices that aren't there."

"And you?" she asked, jiggling the basket at him, her voice drifting already half lost in some other place. "What will you see?"

His mouth twitched, a flicker of wry humor in his eyes. "That's the question, isn't it?" He murmured. "Whether I decide to wait it out and watch... or join you in the madness."

She laughed then, a soft, bright sound that cut through the night air. "I don't think there's any turning back," she said, her voice just above a whisper though she felt she was yelling. "Not anymore."

Corvan exhaled slowly and took a handful of the berries for himself. He took her hand in his, feeling the warmth of her skin, the faint, sticky trace of berry juice between her fingers.

"Then let's see what truths these berries reveal," he said quietly. He squeezed her hand once, a silent promise, and ate the berries.

Together they let the night unfold, magic, madness, and the shimmering line between them.

Chapter 14

The world unraveled slowly.

Sound came first. Fractured and layered. Birdsong echoed underwater. Leaves laughed as they floated by the windows. The crackling fire stretched into a melody, notes warping into a lullaby that curled around her bones.

Nisrine blinked slowly. The stones around the fireplace multiplied. No. Split. Each one was many, fractaling in all directions like glass spun through time. Each piece shimmered like silver scales, breathing with color that wasn't color at all. Her fingers brushed her own knee, but the sensation felt distant, delayed. Like touching someone else.

On Fallen Wings

Corvan sat beside her but he had layers shifting slightly with every blink. One moment he was cloaked in shadow, antlers rising like bone from his brow. Next, his skin was green and his eyes reflected entire moons.

She reached for his hand again.

Or thought she did.

Her hand never quite moved, yet somehow, it was in his. Or perhaps she imagined it.

"Corvan," she murmured, but the name stretched in her mouth, echoed around them. "Coorrvaan…"

He turned to her slowly, eyes catching the firelight. No, not firelight now, but starlight, gleaming silver and blue. His pupils had widened like hers, his breath slow, heavy.

"Do you feel that?" she whispered, clutching at his fingers as vines of golden light slithered across the floor between them.

He nodded once. "The air's… breathing."

They watched it together, both too still, too reverent. Every plank on the cabin floor lifted slightly, as though caught in a wind they couldn't feel. The trees beyond the window pulsed. Not swaying. Breathing.

The room had no corners anymore. Only curves. And doors she didn't remember opening.

Suddenly, the roof disappeared. Stars spilled across the ceiling, so close she could pluck them like apples. She reached up.

Her fingers brushed one, and it burst swirls of apricot and lavender, soft and warm and full of memory.

She gasped. "I saw my mother."

Corvan turned sharply toward her. "What did you see?"

"She was standing beneath a tree," Nisrine said, her voice raw. "The same tree I used to sit under in the gardens. But it was… taller. Older. She was younger than I ever remember. And she smiled at me like she knew I'd come here." Her throat caught. "She said…'You were never meant to stay caged.'"

Corvan didn't speak. He simply reached forward and touched the side of her face, brushing a tear she hadn't realized had fallen.

"Your turn," she whispered, leaning into his touch. "What do you see?"

He hesitated.

Then: "Snow."

She blinked. "Tell me more."

"Snow falling over a ruined city. Empty. Silent. But something… alive beneath it. Magic, buried like bones. I think I've seen this before. In dreams."

The stars above them pulsed in rhythm with their breath. The cabin was gone now, replaced by open sky and endless trees lit with threads of violet and gold. Birds of flame danced through the branches. No, not birds. Memories. They looped overhead, flickering with snatches of voices, music, laughter. Giant moths the size of their palms flitted past, their wings bearing runes that shimmered and changed as they flew. The moon had multiplied, three of them now. One red, one silver, and one that flickered in and out of existence

Nisrine stood, though her feet barely touched the ground. She felt light. Weightless.

She turned and Corvan was right there, mirroring her. His cloak now a shadow of black feathers. His eyes silver-bright.

"You look…" she began, then stopped. "Not different. Just… true."

He tilted his head. "And you're glowing."

She looked down. "Oh."

Her veins shimmered with light, tracing through her skin like rivers of moonfire. Her fingertips sparkled with threads of gold and green. Her heartbeat echoed in her ears like a drum from the deep earth.

"I think I understand now," she said.

"Understand what?"

"What it means to be Fae. What she meant when she said '*The oldest places remember us, even when we forget ourselves.* '" She turned in a slow circle, arms out, eyes wide. "This place. It's not a hallucination. Not really. It's memories. It's magic showing us what's been waiting."

Corvan stepped closer, a breath away. "Then what do you see when you look at me?"

She didn't hesitate. "Someone who remembers. Someone who chose to remember when forgetting would have been easier."

His expression flickered, something like pain, something like gratitude.

The stars above them pulsed, not with danger, but with rhythm. Like a song. A heartbeat. A thread that stitched her to this place, and to him, in a way she couldn't explain, only feel.

The wind picked up again, but this time it wasn't strange or sharp. It was warm, full of scent and story. Of forest moss, lightning storms, and something older. An echo of wild things unafraid to bloom in ruins.

Nisrine exhaled slowly, and the air shimmered with it.

For a long time, neither of them spoke. They just stood together beneath the velvet sky, stars trailing across their shoulders like falling petals.

Nisrine reached for another memory and caught it: her mother's voice saying her name like a blessing. *Nisrine*.

And then, quiet.

The hallucination faded not like a shutter but like the tide retreating. Gentle and reluctant.

Her skin stopped glowing. The stars quieted. Leaves no longer laughed. It didn't feel empty. Only hushed. As though every tree, leaf, and rock had witnessed something sacred.

Corvan's hand found hers, and this time, she knew it wasn't imagined.

"We'll remember this, won't we?" she asked, her voice low.

His fingers tightened around hers. "We'd be fools not to."

And as the walls of the cabin returned around them, solid and real, their joined hands didn't let go.

Chapter 15

The storage cellar beneath the abandoned granary warmed as Seren lit candles. He stood, arms crossed over his chest, eyes fixed on the creaking door at the top of the stairs. He hated using the granary. It was too exposed. Too vulnerable. But it was the only place left in the palace grounds that hadn't been quietly mapped and monitored by Lonan's new surveillance wards.

Olesia slipped in, her footsteps light and quiet. She gave him a nod, confirming what he already suspected. "He sent another," she murmured, her voice barely audible. "Thalen, this time. Gone before dawn. No one's seen him since."

A muscle twitched by Seren's eye. Thalen was barely twenty. A new recruit, eager and kind, with a younger sister still training in the kitchens. Lonan was growing reckless. Or desperate.

The sound of murmurs and shifting cloaks filled the cellar as the others arrived one by one. The healer, Mirell, always wore her hood too low, as if afraid of being recognized, even down here. The spellcasters, Lexa and Axel, arrived together as usual, their twin silver circlets glinting faintly beneath their cloaks. Behind them came Bren, the scout, sharp-eyed and twitching like a hare near a snare, and Caelis, the archivist, already clutching a leather-bound book of forbidden histories.

Captain Aeron followed next, grim-faced and broad-shouldered, with two of his men from the outer patrol close behind, Ruun and Elven, who had risked their positions the moment they chose to follow Aeron instead of the king.

Seren waited until the cellar door thudded shut again, bolted from the inside.

Then silence.

All eyes turned to the figure standing near the back of the room. The newest recruit.

"Riven," Olesia said softly, stepping forward. "Thank you for coming."

The young male looked wary, his posture stiff. His armor bore no crest, just simple dark leather. A sign he had already stripped it of allegiance. "I'm not here to make promises," he said, voice clipped. "Only to hear you out."

Seren stepped into the flickering lamplight. "That's all we ask."

The tension in the air was sharp as a blade. Riven scanned their faces. "I heard rumors. The king is forcing guards through the gate. That he's building something... monstrous."

"He is," Olesia said, and her voice no longer held fear, only conviction. "He's unraveling. And Nisrine... She's not the enemy. She left because she had no choice."

"She was our heir," Seren added, stepping forward. "She was born to lead. But Lonan didn't want a successor. He wanted a bird in a cage."

Caelis opened his book and laid it gently on a crate. "These pages were hidden beneath the royal archives," he said. "They contain accounts of the early years after the gate was sealed. The king struck deals to consolidate power. He rewrote history. Entire bloodlines were erased, villages buried, truths twisted."

Axel lifted a hand, magic sparking faintly along his fingertips. "And now he's sending soldiers to die in a world he refused to teach us about. If we don't act, Nisrine won't survive whatever he sends next. And if she falls," he looked to the others, "so does the last hope of healing either realm."

Silence fell again, heavy with what none of them wanted to say aloud. That they had all waited too long. That maybe it was already too late.

Riven shifted his weight, eyes narrowing. "So, what exactly do you want from me?"

"To be our final sword," Aeron said, voice low. "We're not trying to stage a coup. Not yet. But if we lose track of her, or if Lonan finds a way to control her... we need someone fast, smart, loyal to truth, not blood. I've seen you train. You're good. You'd be better with purpose."

Julie Nelson

Riven looked around the circle again. At Mirell, who had once healed refugees from the borderlands. At the twin casters, whose family had been silenced for speaking against the crown. At Seren, whose silence had allowed the princess to disappear… but whose silence was now a shield turned blade.

"Why now?" Riven asked. "Why not years ago?"

Seren's voice stayed steady. "Because back then, we were still trying to believe in the peace we were told existed. Now we know better."

Riven considered that. For a long moment, he said nothing.

Then he slowly unbuckled the strap across his chest and let his cloak fall open.

Beneath it, a blade rested against his back. Not the curved blades of the royal guard, but one made of old iron, etched with runes that hadn't been spoken aloud in a hundred years.

"If I do this," he said, "we do it clean. No blood unless it's taken from us first."

"You have our word," Olesia said, stepping forward, offering her hand.

He took it.

The candles flickered.

And with them, the quiet rebellion became something else entirely. No longer a resistance of conscience, but a force in motion.

On Fallen Wings

Days later, the storage cellar beneath the abandoned granary had been compromised. Seren didn't dare point fingers at any of his rebel team. But he couldn't help but wonder if there was a traitor in the mix.

The old watchtower had long since fallen out of use, its stones moss-covered, its once-proud banners faded to ghosts in the dim torchlight. But tonight, it pulsed with life again. Quiet, careful life. Seren stood near the broken hearth, arms heavy at his sides, watching as each member of their rebellion filed into place.

Olesia was already there, unrolling the faded parchment on the table she had shown days ago. It was Queen Cherith's writing, pulled from the hidden archive only the archivist, Caelis, had dared preserve.

The healer, Mirell, lingered by the door, her fingers twitching with unease. Across from her, both spellcasters, their magic raw and edged, stood shoulder to shoulder. Captain Aeron leaned on the old stone window frame, every inch the war-hardened soldier, but his gaze was locked on the script before them. The two outer patrol guards remained silent but present, eyes sharp in the torchlight.

And now the final recruit, Lira, the former starlight courier, sat cautiously on a stool, her braid trailing like a rope down her back. She was younger than most of them, but she'd already smuggled forbidden messages between border courts and evaded half a dozen of Lonan's shadow scouts.

"She'll do," Aeron said quietly after a long moment, watching her test the edge of a dagger in the firelight.

Olesia nodded. "She's faster than anyone I've seen. We'll need that."

Seren stepped forward at last. "We all know why we're here. Lonan's losing what little reason he had left. He's forcing guards through the gate now, unprepared, unarmed, some of them wounded before they even cross. And we still don't know what lies beyond."

"Or if they've survived," Mirell murmured.

Seren met each of their eyes in turn. "We can't stop him from this side. Not unless we give Nisrine a way back. Or at least, a way to stay hidden from him long enough to gather allies. That means using the second tether."

Caelis unrolled the second scroll. Thinner, newer parchment covered in intricate diagrams and Cherith's delicate script. "It's not a bridge. It's a bond. A thread of stabilized magic between one soul and another. Queen Cherith theorized it was possible to anchor a tether to a person instead of a place."

"Which would let us... What exactly?" Riven asked. "Send magic through it?"

"More than that," Caelis said. "We could guide her. Protect her. Channel energy if she's in danger. Even... speak to her, if we tune it right."

"That's what she was working on before she vanished," Olesia said quietly. "A way to protect Nisrine. A bond that could stretch across the gate. She just never had time to finish it."

"Then we'll finish it," Seren said. "We have spellcasters. We have a healer. We have everything she didn't have since she had to watch what she did in front of Lonan."

Aeron narrowed his eyes. "Everything except a clear anchor."

Seren did not even hesitate, "I'll be the anchor."

"No." Olesia's voice cut sharply through the room. "It should be me."

"You can't," he started, but she stepped forward, one hand flat against the table.

"She knows me. She trusts me. And I know her rhythm. I was at her side every day. My magic is quieter, but it's steady. That's what a tether needs."

"Both of you," Mirell said slowly, "might be needed. It may not hold with only one link given the distance."

Caelis tapped the diagram. "The queen's theory did suggest multiple threads. A braid of sorts. That might keep it more stable."

Silence fell, broken only by the crackle of the torch.

Finally, Aeron spoke. "Then you do it together. The sooner the better. Lonan's began purging the southern barracks. Anyone who speaks against him disappears."

"We'll need to cast from a neutral space," Lexa said. "Somewhere shielded. Outside the court's boundary."

"I know a place," Riven declared. "There's a hollow grove near the starfall cliffs. Old ground. Sleeping magic. No one goes there anymore."

Caelis nodded. "Perfect. But we'll need to gather the components. Bloodstone, mirrored water, feather ash."

"I'll get the feather ash," Lira offered. "I know where the runemoths shed."

Olesia looked at her, a flicker of something like admiration passing through her eyes. "You really are fast," she said, a small wry smile pulling at her lips.

Lira just nodded, her jaw set. "I'm in," she said, and met Seren's gaze with a fierceness that seemed to echo the quiet resolve in her voice. "Whatever it takes."

Seren exhaled, his breath catching in the hush that followed. Around them, the room seemed to shift, no longer just a shadowed corner of the keep, but a place where purpose took shape. The air thrummed with it, soft and electric. Doubt gave way to resolve, and he could feel it settling in their bones.

"Then we begin tomorrow night," he said, his voice low but sure. "Prepare quietly. Speak to no one. And if any of you are questioned…"

"They won't get a word out of me," Aeron said flatly, his hand resting on the hilt of his dagger like a silent vow.

Seren nodded, grateful for the unspoken loyalty that glimmered in Aeron's eyes.

"One more thing," Olesia added, her fingers brushing over Cherith's script, her voice low but firm. "This magic. It binds more than just distance. If it works…" her brow furrowed, eyes narrowing, "We'll be connected to her in ways even she might not expect. Be ready for that."

Seren swallowed hard. He thought of Nisrine, her grief, her determination, and prayed to whatever gods still listened in this broken world that the bond they forged would be enough to reach her.

Because the king was hunting her.

And they were running out of time.

Chapter 16

Nisrine stood in the clearing, her breath steady, eyes closed, and hands poised. The air was thick with anticipation, the kind that precedes a significant shift.

Corvan observed from a distance, his arms crossed, leaning against a moss-covered tree. He had seen her progress over the past days. Her grasp of ancient magics, her adaptability, and her resilience. But today was different. Today, she would confront the raw essence of her power.

"Begin," he called out.

Nisrine opened her eyes, revealing a determination that hadn't been there before. She extended her right hand, fingers splayed, and murmured an incantation in the old tongue.

"Thyren val'shae, korath drien'thel." The ground beneath her responded, a soft glow emanating from the earth, swirling around her feet.

With a swift motion, she directed the energy upward, forming a protective barrier that shimmered like a heat haze. Sweat beaded on her forehead, but she maintained the spell, refining its edges, stabilizing its core.

Corvan nodded appreciatively. "Good. Now, channel that energy into your blade."

She reached for the training sword at her side. It was a weighted replica designed to mimic the balance of a real weapon. Drawing it, she felt the familiar hum of magic intertwining with the steel. She swung the blade in a wide arc, releasing the stored energy in a burst that sliced through the air, leaving a trail of luminescence.

"Again," Corvan instructed.

She repeated the motion, each swing more precise, more controlled. The fusion of magic and martial skill was no longer a concept but a reality she could wield.

After an hour, Corvan approached. "Rest. You've done well."

Nisrine sheathed her sword, breathing heavily. "I can go on."

He placed a hand on her shoulder. "Pushing too hard can lead to mistakes. Remember, mastery isn't achieved in a day."

She nodded, acknowledging his reasoning.

They sat by a nearby stream, the water's gentle babble providing a soothing backdrop.

"When I first arrived, I was lost," she admitted. "But now, I feel... connected."

Corvan smiled. "You've embraced both sides of yourself. The magic and the warrior. Few can claim such balance."

She looked at him, eyes reflecting the sunlight. "Thank you for guiding me."

He met her gaze. "It's been my honor."

The forest had grown darker.

Not just from the dusk bleeding through the trees or the clouds gathering overhead, but from something else. Something unnatural. The air, usually alive with birdsong and rustling leaves, now held a taut, breathless stillness.

Nisrine stood in the training circle still. Her training sword now hung at her hip. Her fingers grazed its hilt as she scanned the tree line.

Corvan instructed, "Breathe before you strike. Feel the rhythm. Swordplay isn't just skill. It's listening."

They'd trained hard daily. Her arms ached from repetition, but her mind felt clearer than it ever had. Her magic had begun to respond with more ease, too. Not wild bursts, but deliberate, graceful movements, like water drawn from a spring instead of from a storm.

But now, now something felt off.

Corvan, a few steps ahead of her, stilled completely. His eyes narrowed toward the west.

"What is it?" she asked.

"Someone's here," he murmured.

A heartbeat later, a shrill note rang out through the trees. A hunting horn. High-pitched. Grim.

Nisrine's blood went cold. That sound had haunted her dreams.

"The king's guard," she said.

"Two," Corvan confirmed, his voice low. "Coming fast."

A crash echoed closer to them.

"We need to…" he started.

"No," she said firmly. "Let me face them."

Corvan turned sharply to her. "You're not ready for this. A real fight is not like training."

"I *am* ready," she said, voice steady. "I have to be."

Before he could argue further, figures broke from the underbrush. Two of them. Black armor gleamed and silver pauldrons etched with the unmistakable crest of Lonan's Royal Guard.

One veered straight toward Corvan with a sharp cry, twin daggers flashing. The other stopped just short of Nisrine. His helm obscured his face entirely, but something about his stance, rigid, tense, reluctant, gave her pause.

"Princess," he said, voice rough and distorted, like frost cracking against fire. "It's time to go."

Nisrine stepped forward, drawing her blade in a smooth, practiced motion. "I'm not returning."

The guard hesitated. Just for a breath.

Then he lunged. Fast, brutal, like a weapon being wielded by someone else. Their blades met with a sharp, metallic clang. The force of it shuddered through her bones, but she pivoted, letting his momentum carry past her. Just like Corvan had taught her. She slashed across his side. A glancing blow, but it earned a grunt of pain and a step back.

From the corner of her eye, she caught Corvan moving like smoke, dodging and striking with surgical precision. His opponent was fast, relentless. Their fight darted between trees, steel sparking with every clash.

Nisrine focused. Her opponent was strong, but his movements weren't smooth. There was something off. Like he was being controlled, his body reacting by force, not instinct.

He came at her again, and this time their blades locked. He shoved against her, and she let the pressure build. Then slipped out from beneath it, twisting low. Her blade caught his thigh. He staggered.

A dagger flashed in his hand.

Nisrine's instinct took over. The air rippled. Her magic bent it into a shield. The blade ricocheted into the grass.

She stared at her hand. Steady. Controlled. She had done it. Truly done it.

The guard took a step forward, but vines erupted from the earth, coiling around his legs. His breathing was ragged.

She approached, sword raised.

"I don't want to kill you," she said. "But I won't go back. Tell the king I'm not his to command."

"You don't know what he did to me," the guard rasped. His voice cracked mid-sentence, and the anger drained from it. "I didn't want to find you. I didn't. He twisted something in me. I can feel it burning."

Nisrine froze. Her heart skipped a beat.

She stepped closer, raising her blade. Not to strike, but to flick away the helmet.

It clattered to the ground.

The Fae male beneath was young. Too young. Sandy-blonde hair, blood matted. Eyes wide and rimmed with darkness. But not cruelty. Pain.

Her breath caught. "Thalen?"

He gave a shuddering nod, his mouth drawn tight, trembling with the effort to speak "I tried to fight it. I did. I didn't want this."

"I remember you," she said quietly, lowering her sword. "You trained with Seren."

"I wanted to serve the realm," he choked out. "Not... not this."

She knelt beside him as the vines loosened.

"He's using you," she said. "But he doesn't own you."

Tears cut tracks through the grime on his face. "It's inside me. I can feel it. It wants me to finish this."

Nisrine raised her hand, glowing now with purpose. "Then let me burn it out."

Thalen held her gaze, then bowed his head.

Her magic surged forward. Not with violence, but with clarity. A ribbon of light poured from her hand and sank into his chest. He cried out, back arching, before the darkness in his eyes flickered and faded.

Then he slumped forward, unconscious but breathing.

Nisrine exhaled, shaking. Her sword hand trembled. Blood ran down her arm from a shallow wound, but she barely felt it. Her legs shook beneath her, not from fear, but from everything that had just passed through her.

The brush rustled. Corvan emerged, streaked with dirt and blood but standing. His eyes swept over the scene: Nisrine, unconscious guard, the faintly glowing vines still twisting at the edges of the clearing.

"I killed mine," he said, voice low, unreadable. "What do we do with yours?"

Nisrine's gaze didn't leave Thalen's unconscious form. The bruised magic still clung to him like smoke, but it was no longer consuming him. Just residue.

"He sent someone young. This is Thalen. I know him. Willing, but... not in control." She said quietly. "He didn't want to be my enemy. Not really."

"Maybe not," Corvan said, "but Lonan's starting to run out of patience."

She lifted her eyes to the canopy above. The stars were beginning to pierce the darkness, cold and remote.

"I felt it," she murmured. "His magic. It was rushed. Crude. He's pushing them harder. Faster."

"Which means he's afraid."

Nisrine lowered her sword, finally letting her arms relax. "Good."

The forest was still again, but not silent. Her blood hummed with magic that was no longer wild and erratic, but anchored. Watching. Waiting.

Corvan stepped beside her, his voice low. "Desperation makes kings reckless."

She looked at him, and for a moment, her face was fierce with something that went deeper than resolve.

"Let him be reckless," she said. "I'm not running anymore."

They didn't linger. Corvan hefted Thalen's unconscious form over his shoulder with a grunt, moving through the forest paths with silent efficiency. Nisrine followed close behind, her own limbs aching, her cut bandaged but throbbing with every step.

The night deepened around them, the canopy overhead shifting with faint breezes that smelled of pine and damp earth. Somewhere distant, an owl called, low and steady.

They were nearly back home before Thalen stirred, a faint groan breaking the hush. Corvan adjusted his grip, setting him down gently against a fallen log. Thalen's eyes fluttered open, unfocused at first, then cleared as he saw Nisrine.

"Princess," he rasped, shame and gratitude mingling in the word.

She knelt beside him, brushing a leaf from his shoulder. "Easy," she said. "You're safe now."

Thalen's hands curled into fists. "I don't want to go back," he blurted out. The words tumbled from him, raw and shaking. "Please. I can't go back to him."

Nisrine's heart pulled tight. "You won't," she told him, voice steady. "No one here will force you."

His throat bobbed as he swallowed hard. "I trained for the crown. For the realm. For you." He coughed, tears bright in his lashes. "But when Lonan... what he did to me, I thought I could fight it. I tried. Every day."

Corvan watched in silence, a flicker of sympathy in his eyes.

Thalen pressed on, desperation spilling out of him. "I don't care what I have to do. I'll serve you, Princess. I'll give everything. Just don't make me go back."

Nisrine placed a hand on his, warm with her magic. "Your loyalty is yours to give," she said softly, "and I would be honored to accept it."

He bowed his head, shoulders shaking with quiet relief. "Then I'll serve you," he whispered, almost breaking. "To the end."

Corvan stepped forward, setting a steady hand on Thalen's shoulder. "Easy friend," he said, calm and certain. "You'll have your chance to prove it."

Chapter 17

Moonlight spilled in slats between the tree limbs, illuminating the old stones that ringed the clearing. Moss clung to their sides like forgotten names. The trees stood like sentinels around the grove, their branches arching high and silent as cathedral beams.

It was sacred ground.

Seren knelt near the center of the grove, fingers brushing the dirt. The air here was thick with something older than time. Residual magic that stirred just beneath the surface, waiting to be claimed. He could feel it in his bones, in the thrum of the warding stones beneath his boots.

The others arrived one by one.

Olesia approached with the mirrored water, held carefully in a moonstone basin. Beside her, Caelis clutched a bundle of scrolls and crystal fragments. Axel and Lexa carried the bloodstone, veined crimson shards humming with volatile energy, and Merill brought the carved sigils etched into bonewood tiles. Captain Aeron took up watch at the outer rim with Riven, keeping a perimeter in case any of Lonan's spies followed.

Lira arrived last, breathless and dusted with silver powder. "The feather ash," she said, offering a tiny satchel. "Straight from the moth cliffs."

Seren took it gently. "You did well."

She grinned and winked. "Still fast."

They moved wordlessly after that, each member falling into practiced coordination. Olesia and Caelis set the ritual circle, tracing Queen Cherith's diagram into the earth with threads of white chalk and ground quartz. The pattern spiraled outward, ending in nine rune-points, each assigned to a specific element, a purpose, a soul.

"I've never cast something this old," Lexa whispered as she lit the woven incense rope and pressed it into the southern mark.

"Let's just not die," Lira added, crouching next to the feather ash sigil.

Olesia knelt across from Seren, the mirrored basin between them. "Are you ready?" she asked.

Seren didn't answer right away. He looked up, past the trees, past the rising stars, to where he thought Nisrine might be. Somewhere far from here. Somewhere alone.

"I'm ready."

Caelis placed the final relic in the center: a small silver locket, once Cherith's, containing a strand of Nisrine's hair. It glowed faintly in the light. A remnant of the queen's love. The magic needed that. A root to cling to.

Axel touched the water. "Begin."

They spoke in unison, voices rising and falling in the cadence of old Fae. Magic not only cast, but sung into being. The runes flared to life. Light rippled through the circle. The basin shimmered, then deepened, becoming a mirror not just of light, but of distance.

Seren's vision tunneled. He felt her, the familiar shape of her presence, flickering somewhere across the veil. Not close, not yet. But real.

"She's out there," he said softly. "I can feel her."

Olesia reached across the water, her fingers brushing his. "Focus on the tether. See the thread. Not where it leads. Just *that* it leads."

He closed his eyes.

In the darkness behind his lids, a thread emerged. Gossamer-thin. Gold-tinged. Unstable. He grasped for it, not with his hands, but with his intent. His magic. His memory of Nisrine.

Her laughter, sharp and bright in the palace courtyard.

The way she used to braid wildflowers into his armor before hunts.

The night she slipped through the gate and he didn't stop her.

Emotion surged. Too strong.

The tether frayed.

"Seren," Lexa's voice came steady from her sigil. "Center. Emotions shape the weave, but they cannot control it."

He exhaled. Slowed. Let the sorrow slide behind the memory. He opened himself again, softer this time. Not reaching, not grasping, just allowing.

The tether began to hold.

Then, Olesia added hers. Her magic spiraled like a river. Calm, silver, constant. It wound around Seren's strand, interlacing. Not overtaking. Supporting.

Caelis whispered the binding phrases, and the others focused their energy into the circle, feeding the structure. The bloodstone cracked, releasing a red mist that laced the air. The mirrored water turned opaque.

And in the center, the silver locket pulsed once.

Twice.

A third time.

The magic locked.

Then came the backlash.

The circle surged with light. Too much, too fast. The stones around them groaned. The earth buckled slightly beneath the strain. Lexa fell to one knee, her mouth open in a silent cry as her spell form overloaded.

"Steady!" Axel barked, gripping her arm.

The mirror shattered. Not the basin, but the image in it. A flood of heat and wind burst from the center, knocking several of them backward. Lira yelped, catching herself on the mossy roots. Olesia fell, gasping.

But Seren didn't move.

He stood at the heart of the storm, palms open, body rigid, tether blazing in both hands. The connection had opened fully, and it was *alive*.

He could feel Nisrine on the other end. Confused. Asleep, maybe. Or dreaming. But her soul flickered in tandem with his own now, echoing like a heartbeat against his ribcage.

And she was in pain.

He collapsed to his knees, gasping. "She's hurt."

Olesia crawled to him, clutching her side. "You saw her?"

"No, but, I *felt* her."

Caelis steadied the basin, now cracked at the base. "The tether held. That was the worst of the surge."

"Worst *so far*," Axel muttered.

Aeron stepped forward from the tree line. "Did it work?"

Seren looked up slowly. "Yes. We're linked now. It's weak, but it's real."

Mirell pressed a stone into his hand. "Then let us strengthen it before it fades."

One by one, they each touched the remaining sigils, feeding their essence into the weave. Not overpowering it, just anchoring it. Giving the tether ground to cling to.

It was ancient, imperfect magic.

But it was hope.

By dawn, the circle was dark again, the grove silent but forever changed.

They didn't speak as they left, each filing back into the world one by one, their roles unchanged but their purpose sharpened.

And Seren, heart still humming with the beat of another soul, knew exactly what had to happen next.

Nisrine had a tether now. But she would also need an army.

Nisrine stood in a field of night-blooming lilies. They shimmered beneath a silver sky, each petal pulsing gently, like they breathed with her. The world around her was hushed, as though sound had folded inward. No breeze, no birdsong, only the hush of starlight.

She felt weightless. Rootless. Alone, but not in a frightening way.

Not this time.

She took a step, bare feet brushing dew-drenched grass. The air smelled faintly of lemon and myrrh.

"Where am I?" she asked aloud, but her voice didn't echo. It vanished the moment it left her lips.

Then, she felt it, a tug, faint but unmistakable, in her chest. As if a silken thread had been knotted around her ribs. It pulled softly, not demanding, not dragging. Just... anchoring.

Julie Nelson

Nisrine stilled, hand resting over her heart. The tug pulsed again. Warmer this time. Familiar.

A flood of memories surfaced. Seren's voice at her back in the forest. Olesia's steady hands braiding her hair before court. Captain Aeron, teaching her how to map stars. Her mother's touch, long gone but never forgotten.

The tether pulled again, and suddenly the lilies blurred, the sky shifted, and she felt herself *falling* through the dream.

But she didn't wake.

Instead, she landed gently in a space filled with light, not blinding, but radiant, golden, humming. The thread in her chest glowed now, visible, connecting her to something far away.

Or *someone*.

She turned, and though she saw no one, she *felt* him. Seren.

He wasn't speaking. But she felt the impression of his thoughts brushing against hers. Worry. Guilt. Hope.

She blinked, her throat tight. "Seren?"

The connection flickered, just briefly.

The pain she hadn't realized she'd been carrying began to ebb. The magic inside her, usually wild and restless, settled into something quieter. Steadier. As if a second heartbeat had joined hers and brought her into rhythm.

She sat slowly on the grass of this imagined space and closed her eyes.

And when she finally woke, the thread remained.

Faint. Fragile.

But unbroken.

148

Chapter 18

Candlelight flickered against the walls of the hidden chamber beneath the armory, shadows danced over old stone and nervous faces. A map of the realms stretched across the table, marked in charcoal and ink, dotted with sigils from Queen Cherith's stolen notes. Around it, the rebels leaned in, twelve strong now, each bound by shared loyalty and growing desperation.

Captain Aeron adjusted his gauntlet with a grimace. "Lonan's losing what little reason he had. He forced three more scouts through the gate yesterday. Two haven't come back."

"He's hunting her like she's the enemy," Mirell whispered, her voice tight. "She's just a girl."

"No." Seren's voice cut through the murmurs. "She's more than that now. And had a feeling this moment would come. We've spent too long waiting. Tonight, we act."

Olesia nodded beside him, arms crossed over her chest. "We need to set the second tether before the king's next purge. We can't risk more eyes on us."

They turned to Caelis, who gently unrolled the parchment copied from Queen Cherith's journal. Faint, delicate runes curled along its edges like vines. The spell, half memory, half miracle, was a design the queen had never dared complete. A second tether. A magical echo of the gate's pulse, drawn through intention.

"It'll need a binding focus," Caelis murmured, pointing to a symbol on the page. "One of you has to carry it. Someone close to her."

Everyone looked at Seren.

He met their eyes without hesitation. "She marked me once," he said. "Years ago. A charm on a thread, before her royal trials. Her mother said it meant trust."

Bren raised a brow. "You kept it?"

Seren drew the thin chain from beneath his armor. The thread had frayed, but the small carved charm with both of their blood dried to it still pulsed faintly with Fae magic. "Of course I kept it."

Olesia's expression softened, then hardened again. "This is our only shot."

Seren stepped away from the table, breath steadying. The others quieted as he knelt, placing the charm against the ground. He closed his eyes, drawing on the memory of Nisrine, her laughter, her fury, her impossible hope. He focused on the thread of her magic, the one that still echoed faintly in his mind.

He whispered her name into the stone. "Nisrine."

The second tether ignited, a faint golden line running from the charm across the chamber floor. Not visible to most eyes, but Seren felt it hum like a heartbeat, like wings ready to beat.

And through that thread, his thoughts stretched outward, carried on the current that once only Queen Cherith could wield.

You were never meant to run alone, Nis. You were meant to lead.

Show us the way. We will come to you.

Nisrine jolted upright, her breath caught in her throat.

The forest outside Corvan's cottage was still cloaked in dusk, the moon just a sliver above the tree line. But something had changed in the air. Not the usual whisper of magic, not the dream-like hum of the old rituals Corvan had been teaching her. This was different. Intimate. Intentional. Like a thread had just been pulled taut inside her chest.

She pressed a hand over her heart, and there it was again: a voice. Distant, but clear. Familiar.

You were never meant to run alone, Nis. You were meant to lead.

Her eyes widened.

"Seren," she whispered.

She could still feel the charm she had given him. A small blessing of protection on a carved stone. But now the magic she had woven into it thrummed to life, a beacon of warmth in the dark. The connection hadn't broken after all this time. It had waited.

Then, another thread of thought surged across the tether.

Show us the way. We will come to you.

Nisrine stood abruptly, knocking aside the fur blanket from her shoulders. Her knees nearly gave, still weak from the day's training, but the magic inside her had surged with new energy. Urgency.

She stumbled to the door and yanked it open. The wind greeted her with a sharp breath of pine.

Corvan was outside, tending the edge of the fire pit, brow furrowed in thought. He looked up as soon as she emerged. "Nisrine?"

"I felt it." Her voice came out half breathless, half elated. "He reached me. Seren. I don't know how, but he did it. He wants me to show the way here. They're coming."

Corvan froze. His shoulders stiffened, the blood draining from his face. "No."

Nisrine blinked. "What?"

"You can't." He crossed to her quickly, his expression carved from fear. "You have no idea what else that could unleash."

"I do," she insisted, eyes alight. "I know it's dangerous. But he's trying to help me. He *believes* in me."

Corvan grabbed her arms, not roughly, but firmly. "Nisrine, listen to me. That gate is more than a barrier. It's a seal. A lock on something ancient. Something even the Fae stopped trying to control."

She flinched at the intensity in his voice.

"You don't understand what's buried beneath it. The gate doesn't just separate worlds. It holds back the *remnants* of old magic. Creatures. Things that don't follow our rules anymore. Monsters born when the veil first tore."

Nisrine shook her head. "But my people. Seren...."

"And what happens if they walk through and the whole structure collapses?" he asked. "Do you think Lonan will stop with the few he's already sent? You'll bring him here, Nisrine. You'll bring all of them. And they'll bring war with them."

Tears stung at the corners of her eyes. "So what do I do, Corvan? Just leave them behind? Leave *him* behind?"

His hands fell away from her shoulders. "I don't want that. But I want you to survive more."

She looked down, lips quivering slightly. The magic inside her was still glowing, still reaching across that invisible thread toward Seren's call. It wanted to act. It wanted to respond.

But Corvan was right. If the gate broke, there would be no undoing it. There was no telling how fragile it had become between her passes and whatever Lonan was doing to it.

Nisrine turned away, her voice barely a whisper.

"I won't do it. Not yet."

Corvan let out a quiet breath, as though he'd been holding it the entire time.

And beneath her skin, the tether still pulsed, steady, waiting.

Chapter 19

Morning dawned quietly, but the air felt wrong.

Nisrine moved through the small cottage kitchen in slow, automatic motions. She broke eggs into a pan, added wild herbs they'd foraged together days ago, and stirred until the mixture formed into something edible. Her hands moved on their own, but her thoughts weren't in the room.

The tether still pulsed beneath her skin.

It hadn't stopped all night. A quiet drumbeat. A distant heartbeat echoing from Seren's side of the world, like a question that hadn't been answered.

She hadn't sent a reply.

Behind her, Corvan stirred awake on the other side of the main room. He murmured a groggy greeting, rubbed his eyes, and took the cup of tea she handed him without a word. For a few minutes, they ate in silence at the small table. Only the tinkling of forks on plates and the faint whistle of wind outside filled the space between them.

"You're not really here," Corvan said finally, his voice gentle but certain.

Nisrine looked up sharply.

"I can feel it," he added, setting his tea down. "You're still listening to that call."

She hesitated, then nodded.

Thalen entered the kitchen as quietly as possible.

"I don't know what the right choice is," she whispered. "But I feel like something is unraveling. Like the longer I wait, the more threads I lose. What if he's in danger, Corvan? What if they all are?"

Corvan leaned back, arms folded loosely across his chest. "And what if it's a trap?"

"I would feel that," she said instantly. "Seren wouldn't… He couldn't."

"Seren isn't the bad guy here, Corvan." Thalen finally said while setting his plate down next to Nisrine.

"I know you trust him. But that gate isn't just a doorway. It's a seal." He looked between both of them. Then he looked at Nisrine steadily. "And you are not ready to fight what might come through it."

The words landed hard, but not untrue. She wasn't ready. Not completely. But would she ever be? *And what about Seren? What if he's ready now, and I'm the one holding them back?*

They finished their food in silence. Then, without needing to speak, they rose and went outside to train.

The clearing where they practiced had been shaped over time. Flattened with their footsteps, rimmed by hanging crystals that caught light and hummed with low enchantments. The forest surrounded them on all sides, a wall of green and shadow, but this space had become theirs. Safe. Familiar.

Today, it felt different.

Corvan handed her a practice sword without a word. She wrapped her fingers around the leather hilt, grounding herself in the weight of it. Thalen joined them then. He circled her once, then took his stance across from her.

"Begin," Corvan demanded.

They moved.

Steel met steel with a clash. She pivoted, struck low, blocked high. Thalen pressed harder today, forcing her to adapt, to improvise. She ducked beneath his swing, rolled, and landed a blow against his shoulder.

Corvan grunted. "Good. Again."

They moved through the patterns, faster now. The sword was becoming an extension of her. Her muscles remembered where her mind faltered, and the magic that coiled in her veins hummed with focus instead of fury.

But she was distracted, and Corvan saw it. He took Thalen's place.

"Where are you?" he snapped, knocking her weapon aside.

She hissed, pivoted to recover, but he was already behind her. A sharp press of his blade hilt against her ribs stopped her short.

On Fallen Wings

"Dead. You're dead," he said.

She pulled away with a glare. Thalen suddenly found a rock several feet away very interesting.

"Try again."

She did. Again, and again, each movement burning frustration out of her limbs. Until finally, something shifted.

Corvan struck low, and she didn't think. She *felt*. Magic surged through her heels and into the ground. She flipped backward, narrowly avoiding his swing, then thrust her palm toward him with a cry.

The air cracked.

A blast of controlled wind hurled him back a full three feet. He landed hard, rolled, and came up breathless but grinning.

Nisrine stood panting, hair wild, a shimmer of raw energy sparking at her fingertips. For the first time in days, she wasn't just reacting, she was *commanding*.

"Better," Corvan coughed, brushing dirt from his shoulder.

She smiled faintly.

But the joy faded as soon as she lowered her hand.

The tether pulsed again. Subtle, but undeniable. Waiting. Wanting.

She stepped back, suddenly cold. "They're counting on me."

Corvan's smile fell. The air between them was too full of things neither could fix with magic or blades. Finally, Corvan turned away.

"Come on," he said quietly.

Nisrine didn't move.

She looked toward the horizon instead, past the trees, past the mist, toward the direction where the gate must still stand, still whole. Her heart ached with a choice that offered no mercy, no right answer, only consequence.

The tether pulsed again.

But this time… it wasn't a call.

It was a plea.

The thread remained quiet.

Too quiet.

Seren stood motionless near the edge of the glade where they'd made camp for the night, staring into the windless dark as if he could force the tether to move just by willing it. Nothing. Not even a flicker of response.

It had been hours since he'd pulled on the connection. It was subtle at first, then more urgent. He'd hoped for a rush of warmth or even the faint shimmer of her voice in his mind. But the silence pressed down harder than any battlefield weight.

"She should've answered by now," he muttered.

Behind him, Olesia sat on a moss-draped log, repairing the seam on her glove with methodical needlework. "Maybe she's waiting until it's safe," she offered, not looking up. "Maybe she can't respond."

Seren gave a low, frustrated breath. "Or maybe she won't."

Olesia didn't answer. She didn't have to. They were both thinking the same thing.

Lonan had forced more guards through the gate yesterday.

"She's scared," Olesia said softly after a pause. "That's not weakness. It means she knows what's at stake."

"I know she's scared," Seren snapped, sharper than he meant. Then, softer, "I'm scared too."

He sat down heavily across from her, wiping a hand across his face. Moonlight filtered through the trees in silver strands, casting long shadows that made their small group seem even smaller.

Twelve of them. Twelve rebels against a kingdom.

Olesia set down the glove. Her fingers trembled, just a little.

"I remember the first time I saw her cry," she said suddenly, not looking at him.

Seren blinked. "When?"

"Years ago. She was maybe ten. She'd run off from a court lesson. Some noble had said something cruel about her wings, and she didn't want anyone to see her upset." A small, bitter smile touched her lips. "I found her hiding behind the aviary garden. Knees pulled up, face in her arms. She wouldn't even look at me at first."

Seren tilted his head, watching Olesia closely now.

"I sat with her until she spoke. I thought she was going to tell me what he said, or complain about court life like always." Olesia's gaze went distant. "But instead, she told me she didn't think she belonged. Anywhere. Not in the palace. Not in the wild. She said she wished she could rip her wings off and start over as something else."

A lump formed in Seren's throat. He could picture it too easily. Nisrine small and bright, hurting in silence the way she always had.

Olesia exhaled slowly. "That was the day I swore I'd never leave her side. Not just to protect her from others, but to protect her from herself. Because sometimes the things she thinks make her broken... they're the very things that make her worth fighting for."

Seren's jaw pulled tight with restraint.

He hadn't known that story. He'd seen a thousand sides of Nisrine, from reckless laughter to quiet defiance, but he hadn't seen that moment. He hadn't realized Olesia had, until now.

"She's everything," he said finally, the words cracking a little as they left his chest.

Olesia nodded once. "Which is why we can't let fear stop us now."

They sat in silence again, listening to the rustle of the wind and the distant patrols still loyal to the king. Somewhere beyond the veil of worlds, Nisrine was trying to make a decision that might cost her everything.

And here they were, helpless, waiting.

Seren rose. "I'm going to try again." Olesia stood with him.

He closed his eyes and found the tether again. It hummed beneath his ribs now, barely restrained. He didn't pull this time. He sent her something different.

A memory.

Nis, do you remember the clearing in the northern hills, where we found the broken mirror half-buried in snow?

You said the world looked different when you saw yourself reflected in shards. I told you it didn't matter how broken the mirror was, your light still shone through.

You're that light now. We need you to show us the way. Whatever comes, we'll face it together.

The thread vibrated like a plucked harp string.

Seren opened his eyes and turned to Olesia, who had one hand pressed against her chest. She could feel it too.

"She heard that," Olesia whispered.

"Good," Seren said grimly. "Because it looks like we're out of time."

From the far side of the glade, Aeron appeared, armor half-cloaked, face tight with urgency. "He's moving again," he said. "Lonan's called in the inner circle. I don't know what he's planning, but it's big."

"We need that gate open soon," Bren added as he dropped from the trees. "Otherwise, we'll be buried before we ever reach it."

Seren looked to Olesia.

"We start preparing. Now," he said. "We pack. We mask our trail. And we make sure every last soul in this camp is ready to cross the moment she calls us through."

Olesia nodded and turned to relay instructions, fluid and focused, like a river finding its course. She paused and glanced once more at Seren.

Seren hadn't moved. He stood still beneath the trees, the tether still faintly glowing where it brushed along his collarbone. His features locked with tension, shoulders rigid, as though

161

holding back something sharp. His eyes didn't track the movement of their group. They stared into the distance, into a place no one else could see.

Olesia's breath caught.

She had seen warriors grieve. Seen brothers fall and sisters bury their dead. But this wasn't grief. It was something closer to dread. A weight too heavy to be only about orders or duty or even loyalty to the crown.

No, this was about *her*. About Nisrine.

Olesia understood then. Seren wasn't afraid of losing the rebellion. He was afraid of failing the one person who had never asked him to prove himself. The one person who saw him not as a soldier, not as a protector, but as *Seren*.

A knot formed in Olesia's chest. Not envy. Not even sorrow. Just quiet knowing.

She turned away before he noticed her watching, something solemn settling in her bones. Not a vow, not exactly.

But a choice.

As she moved to rally the others, her steps remained steady.

She didn't say anything.

But the next time she looked at Seren, it was with new understanding, and a vow not unlike his own.

She would follow Nisrine through fire and ruin if she had to.

And she would never let Seren walk that path alone.

Chapter 20

Nisrine paused mid-step in the cottage, her hand frozen over the half-carved rune Corvan had asked her to shape from the bark of the elder tree.

A tug.

No, not a tug. A thread. Familiar, quiet, and thrumming with urgency. It wound through her chest like it belonged there, golden and warm and full of grief.

Seren.

Her breath caught as the tether snapped taut, words woven not in sound but in feeling. In the memory he shared.

Her hands began to tremble. "Something's wrong," she whispered.

From behind her, Corvan looked up. He still had dirt on his hands and a smudge of ash on his forehead. "What is it?"

She turned slowly, clutching the tether like a pulse. "It's Seren. The tether. It flared. He sent a message."

Thalen stood. His eyes narrowed. "What did he say?"

She hesitated. Her throat tightened. "He shared a memory." She didn't feel the need to explain anything more than that.

Corvan's entire body stilled. He knew she was keeping something from him.

"No," he said immediately. "Absolutely not."

Nisrine bristled. "You don't even know…"

"I *do* know. If the gate fails and breaks, everything on this side will feel it. Not just your people." His voice rose, rough with something more than anger. "Do you have any idea what else you might let through?"

"I know what's at risk," she said.

"No, you *don't,*" Corvan shouted as he strode closer, magic sharp in the air around him.

She shook her head. "They're my people, Corvan. My family. They're walking into darkness to find me, and you want me to sit here, pretending we're safe?"

His eyes flashed with a strange intensity. "And you, Princess, are the key to everything. If you unleash the magic within you, if you break the barrier, you'll open the floodgates. And nothing, no one, will be safe."

Nisrine took a step forward to the door, wringing her hands as the decision gnawed at her.

"I need some air," she said softly.

He let her go and did not try to stop her. His sharp gaze lingered as she stepped outside. He knew she would go and open the gate. He just hoped she wouldn't.

Nisrine waited until Corvan's footsteps faded completely. Thalen knew better than to get involved. No creak of floorboards, no rustle of fabric. Just silence. She moved then, careful and deliberate, slipping past the training field and the fallen trees, making her way toward the clearing.

There she found the Fae gate in the location where it had deposited her into this world for a second time. It still hummed faintly with old, forgotten power.

The wind stirred, threading through the trees like whispers. Her fingers found the tether once more. This time, she didn't speak with words. She answered with intent, with the steady fire of her resolve.

"I'm sorry, Corvan," she whispered to the wind. "But they need me."

She closed her eyes.

Thought of Olesia's fierce loyalty. Of Seren's quiet strength. Of the way they had never stopped believing in her, even when she had begun to doubt herself. And then she thought of the palace she'd once called home. The beauty. The perfection. The illusion. A gilded cage built by a king who claimed love while dealing only in control.

She reached for the power sleeping inside her, buried deep in her bones. The ancient Fae magic stirred like a beast uncurling, recognizing its name in her thoughts. Her breath caught as the connection flared to life between herself and the land, between two worlds balanced on a fraying cord.

She felt the barrier then. Cold. Brittle. Hollow. A wall made not just of magic, but of fear.

She reached out.

The moment her magic brushed the edge of the barrier, it reacted. Violently.

The ground vibrated beneath her feet. The stones began to hum a low, resonant tone that climbed her spine and echoed in her ribs. The air warped around her. The boundary strained like glass under too much pressure.

Then, impact.

Magic surged toward her like a tide breaking through a dam. Not gentle, not tame. A wild flood of light and sound, of memory and instinct. Wind howled as it tore through the clearing, pulling at her cloak, her hair, her breath.

The earth cracked, a jagged line around her.

Then, with a sound like crystal shattering under immense weight, the gate broke.

A fissure tore through the air. Jagged, vertical, glowing with a white-blue brilliance like the heart of a star. Lightning arced out in wild veins. Trees groaned. Birds scattered. The forest screamed.

Nisrine shielded her eyes as magic roared through the breach. It wasn't like anything she had imagined. It wasn't beauty or terror, it was both. Creation and destruction, life and death, joy and grief, all in a single breath.

The blast threw her backward.

She hit the ground hard, pain flaring in her shoulder, but she kept her eyes open.

She *had* to see it.

The gate flickered. Stabilized. Glowed. It pulsed like a heartbeat, steady, alive, awake.

The moment the barrier shattered, the world seemed to exhale. The trees swayed as though bowing. The air itself shimmered. Power flooded into the clearing like an unseen tide, saturating every root, every stone, every breath.

Nisrine rose slowly, muscles shaking, her limbs thrumming with energy. She stood in the center of the storm. The sky churned above her, stars flickering like uncertain witnesses. Wind tore through the clearing, full of scent, earth, and ash. Ancient things awakened.

She had never felt anything like it.

The magic was too vast, too wild. It pushed and pulled against her soul. She feared she had made a grave mistake.

But then, something shifted.

It was like recognizing herself in a mirror for the first time. She *was* the storm. She *was* the magic. It wasn't tearing her apart. It was welcoming her home. The power of the Fae, the land, and the worlds beyond had always been within her, waiting for her to acknowledge it, to embrace it.

And so, she did. She didn't fight it. She *claimed* it.

With a forceful breath, Nisrine gathered the energy, bringing it under control. It was a delicate balance, like holding the reins of a wild stallion, but she could feel the magic responding to her as if it had been waiting for her command. A living current of power, held in her hands like fire tamed by will. Then it was done as quickly as it started.

The forest quieted. The stars blinked back into place.

The world had been irrevocably changed. There was no going back.

Behind her, leaves crunched under slow, disbelieving steps.

Nisrine's chest rose and fell, still caught in the aftermath of the storm, as she turned toward the sound. There she saw Corvan and Thalen, watching her with wide eyes and gaping mouths.

He knew she would do it, and they followed her when she didn't realize it. "You've done it," Thalen said quietly, though his voice held an undertone of fear. "You've unleashed it. The barrier is gone. The worlds are connected again."

"I didn't know if I could control it," she admitted, her voice sounding torn. "It was like the magic was… testing me. But I think I've *found* it. I've found the way to channel it."

"But at what cost?" Corvan asked, a quiet tremor of dread threading through his words.

Chapter 21

Seren staggered as the pull of the tether slammed into him like a shockwave.

"She did it," he breathed.

Olesia spun toward him, eyes wide. "She opened it."

"No time." Seren's voice was already turning clipped, sharp with urgency. "Everyone move!"

The others sprang into motion. Captain Aeron was first to the edge of the circle, sword already drawn, though his knuckles were pale. Mirell gripped a satchel tight to her chest, whispering a protective spell over them all. The twins, Axel and Lexa, linked hands, focusing their energy to keep the magic stable. Olesia, Lira, Riven, Ruun, Elven, and Caelis stood shoulder to shoulder ready to go. Bren checked the rear, then gave a terse nod to Seren.

They were ready.

One by one, they stepped into the searing light that pulsed at the center of the circle. It was no longer a gate. It was a puncture in the world, and through it, the other realm bled in.

Seren was the last to go. As his boot crossed the threshold, a sudden force rippled out. A screech of twisting magic like metal torn apart. The barrier resisted. For a heartbeat, it felt like it might swallow him whole.

But then, release.

Behind them, left in the ruins of the broken gate, were wings. Twelve pairs of them. Fae wings, iridescent and fragile, scattered like fallen leaves. Some still glowed faintly. Others had already dulled.

The price of crossing.

He stumbled into the clearing like someone breaking through the surface of deep water, lungs burning with panic and hope.

The air buzzed with wild, untamed magic. The trees around the broken gate leaned away as if recoiling from the force that had just been unleashed. Cracks spiderwebbed across the stones, and where the ancient threshold had once stood firm, only scattered fragments remained. The light had dimmed, but the aftershock of what had happened remained in every twitching leaf, every groaning root.

And there, at the edge of it all, stood Nisrine. Her eyes met his across the distance, bright and aching.

"Seren," she breathed, voice raw with disbelief.

He didn't speak. He couldn't.

He crossed the shattered stones in three long strides and pulled her into his arms like a male who feared he would never again get the chance. His hands gripped her shoulders, then her back, as if trying to convince himself she was real.

"You," his voice cracked, and he pressed his forehead to hers. "You're alive. You're here."

Nisrine clung to him, trembling with exhaustion. "I didn't know if I'd ever see you again," she whispered.

He cupped her face, his thumbs brushing the dirt from her skin. "Don't do that again. Don't make me chase you through two worlds."

She let out a small, broken laugh. "I wasn't sure you'd be able to make it."

His expression turned tender. "I'd tear the veil apart with my bare hands to reach you."

Olesia burst into the clearing, her braid half undone, breath ragged. Her eyes darted around as if expecting danger to lunge from the shadows at any second. Not like a soldier scanning for threats, but like someone who had pushed through fear just to get here.

When her gaze landed on Nisrine, safe and alive in Seren's arms, she let out a sound somewhere between a sob and a laugh. Her shoulders sagged with relief, and she stumbled forward, eyes shining.

"You reckless, wonderful girl," Olesia whispered, voice thick with emotion as she flung her arms around Nisrine. "I thought you were..." Her words broke off. She hugged her tighter. "Don't do that again. Please."

Nisrine buried her face in Olesia's shoulder, the tension she'd carried finally beginning to unravel.

171

Around them circled the others, Captain Aeron with his sharp eyes and rigid posture; Bren, Riven, Ruun, and Elven, lean and quiet, already scanning the trees; Axel and Lexa with wary awe etched into their faces; Caelis clutching Queen Cherith's stolen journal like it might vanish if he blinked; Lira looking equally as disheveled as Olesia; and Mirell, eyes narrowed, already assessing Nisrine for signs of magical blowback.

Olesia stepped away and Seren held onto Nisrine once more.

The moment stretched, alive with magic, grief, hope, and the raw tremble of reunion. Nisrine let herself lean into the moment, just for a breath. The warmth of Seren's arms, the thrum of his pulse beneath her fingers. It felt like something steady in the middle of the storm.

Her guard began to slip, just slightly before a loud *crack* split the silence like lightning tearing open the sky. One of the ancient stone markers groaned, a fissure yawning wide across its surface. A scream of bending magic followed, high and metallic. Blue light shot like veins through the trees, rippling outward. The air snapped and buzzed. Every hair on the back of Nisrine's neck lifted.

The gate was still unstable.

And it was leaking.

Seren stepped back. His hands left her arms, but the warmth remained on her skin. He looked at the gate, then looked at her. "You felt it too," he said quietly. "Whatever came through… it wasn't just us, was it?"

She swallowed hard and shook her head once. "No." Her voice barely made it past her lips.

The silence that followed was brittle, straining under the hum of wild magic. Like the land itself held its breath.

Olesia turned, her tone suddenly all business. "We set up a temporary warding. Defensive circle. Anything that comes through next might not be friendly."

"*Will* not be friendly," muttered Riven, already pacing the tree line, his hand on the hilt of his blade.

But Nisrine wasn't listening. Her feet moved of their own accord, carrying her toward the remnants of the gate. Its edges shimmered like a mirage, blurring and reforming with every breath. A pulsing, twisted wound in the fabric of the world. And it was alive.

Behind her, Seren remained still.

He watched her in silence. Watched the girl he'd sworn to protect walk into the very heart of a broken world. The shimmer of the gate cast her in flickering light, and for a heartbeat, he remembered the child she'd been. Wings like stained glass, laugh like summer rain, eyes that used to look only to him for what came next.

She wasn't that girl anymore.

"We didn't know if you'd answer the call," he said softly.

She turned her head at the sound of his voice. Met his eyes with something deep and unreadable. "I almost didn't," she said, her voice steady despite the ache in it.

Something flickered across Seren's face. Regret, pride, grief, maybe all of it. He stepped forward as if to close the space between them again, but she had already turned away.

To *him*.

Corvan stood just beyond the clearing, arms crossed, tension radiating from his frame like a drawn bow. His grey eyes met hers, shadowed with something between concern and resignation. He hadn't said a word since the others arrived.

Every head turned when she did. The Fae warriors. The spellcasters. The healer. The archivist. Even Olesia's expression shifted from relief to wariness.

The silence was different now. Tense, charged. Nisrine felt it like a blade between her shoulders.

Seren's brows furrowed. Olesia's hand dropped near her dagger. Riven took a subtle step to the side. Mirell moved closer to her, unconsciously protective.

Corvan's composure didn't crack.

He stepped into the clearing with calm, deliberate steps, his voice even. "I'm Corvan. I've been helping her survive my world."

He didn't emphasize *my*, but it landed all the same.

Olesia tilted her head, eyes narrowing. "Are you… Fae?"

"Half," he said, unbothered. "But I know more about the old magic than anyone you'll find on this side of the veil."

Nisrine's voice cut gently through the tension. "He warned me not to open the gate. Told me what might come through if I did."

Seren's gaze stayed fixed on Corvan. "And still, she did it."

A flicker of tension crossed Corvan's face, but he nodded. "Because you called her."

No one spoke.

Then Olesia, ever the sharpest blade in any room, gave a slow, assessing nod. "Then I suppose we owe you our thanks. Even if you tried to stop her."

"I didn't stop her," Corvan said. "I stood with her."

Seren was the one to move first. He stepped closer, measuring. Then, slowly, he extended a hand, not entirely in welcome, but in recognition. "Then stand with us now."

Corvan hesitated only a moment before clasping his forearm in return. Thalen emerged at that moment and Seren exhaled, tensions bleeding from his shoulders. He hadn't seen Thalen since just after he graduated training.

Seren stepped forward, gripping Thalen's shoulder with a firm hand. Part relief, part silent reassurance.

"I had hoped you'd be alright." Seren said quietly. "They never should have sent you. But I'm glad you found her."

Thalen managed a weak smile. "You trained me well."

Seren smiled and gave a small nod.

In that moment, Corvan felt a renewed sense of purpose. The path ahead was uncertain, fraught with challenges. But now, Fae and half-Fae, rebels and exiles, all stood united.

The magic still hummed like a struck chord, vibrating through the air and into their bones. The shattered gate loomed behind them. Jagged and wrong, an open wound in the world that refused to close. Light pulsed at its fractured edges, slow and uneven, like a dying heartbeat.

Seren turned to the group, his expression hardening into the familiar lines of command. "We need to move fast. This gate won't stay stable for long, and whatever Lonan's forcing through from the other side may already be tracking us."

Captain Aeron nodded. "We'll need a perimeter, a fallback point if the forest becomes compromised."

"We also need a safe shelter," Mirell added, eyes flicking to Nisrine. "The longer we stay here, the more risk we invite."

Nisrine swayed slightly as she spoke, the edges of her vision dimming just for a breath. The magic still hummed through her like distant thunder, spent but echoing. She exhaled slowly and nodded. "Mirell's right. We can't stay here. This circle, it's a beacon now."

Corvan stepped to Nisrine's side. "There's a hollow east of here. Old trees naturally shielding. I used it while studying the gate. It'll hide us. Let us regroup."

Seren gave him a tight nod. "That will do."

As others spoke, plans forming like bricks in a wall, Nisrine's gaze flicked toward him. Seren felt it before he saw it, like a whisper brushing the edge of his thoughts.

He looked back.

And for a breathless second, they just *looked.* No orders, no mission, no war. Just two souls who had grown up in a world of crowns and oaths and secrets, now standing in the shattered aftermath of everything they thought unbreakable.

He walked to her side. His fingers brushed against hers. Just the lightest touch. Not enough for anyone else to notice. But she felt it. A grounding spark through the fraying storm inside her.

She turned slightly toward him, her hand lingering at her side. She could feel the tension in him. The fear he'd never admit, the grief he kept wrapped in duty. She wanted to reach for him. To say the words they hadn't said back at the gate.

But there was no time.

Aeron spoke again, motioning to the spellcasters. "We'll begin defensive glyphs and tracking wards. Anything that crosses through this spot again, we'll know it."

Caelis stepped forward, clutching Queen Cherith's notes. His voice was low but urgent. "We also need to break Lonan's tether to her. If we don't, he'll keep tracking her."

Olesia frowned. "How do we do that?"

Caelis flipped to a marked page in the worn journal. "The bond was created through blood. A royal bloodline seal. To sever it, we'll need to disrupt the signature it's tied to."

Olesia crossed her arms. "Disrupt it with what? Magic?"

Caelis looked up from the notes, his expression solemn. "With blood. But not just any blood. It has to come from the one the tether was built around. Her blood. Willingly given."

All eyes turned toward Nisrine. She didn't cringe, but just said "Okay."

"No," Corvan said sharply, stepping in as if to block the path before her. His eyes, usually so guarded, burned with a rare intensity. "There has to be another way. That spell is volatile. If it fractures, if it rebounds…"

"She's the only one it *will* work for," Caelis interrupted gently, his voice carrying an edge of sorrow. "Queen Cherith wrote it to tie to her daughter's line. It's old magic. Personal."

"I can do it," Nisrine said. Her voice was low but resolute. "And I *will*. But not here."

Olesia's gaze narrowed. "Then we take the spell with us. Prepare it when we're safe."

Seren's expression had turned stony again, but when his eyes found Nisrine's, something softened there. Barely. His

177

voice was clipped and focused, commanding, but Nisrine heard the care beneath the words. The fragile hope he held tight against the fear. "Two-person scouting team to sweep ahead. No lights, low sound. Riven, Olesia, take them. Corvan, show me the hollow. Thalen, you're with us."

Corvan gave a small nod, his eyes still on Nisrine, as if trying to read her thoughts. "It's about a half-day's walk. But there's a shortcut through the birch valley."

"Then let's not waste time," Seren drew a slow breath, his hand flexing at his side. "We're ghosts now. The king will already know the gate's broken."

"And if he comes?" one of the outer guards, Ruun, asked, his voice carrying the fear they all felt but didn't name.

Nisrine's voice rose from the center of them. Quiet, calm, and sure. "Then we make sure he regrets it."

A hush fell over the clearing. It wasn't fear that settled in, it was resolve. It was the kind of silence that came before a storm, the deep breath before everything changed.

They were no longer scattered. No longer half-hidden behind whispered plans and fleeting hopes. In that moment, they were one.

As the dying light spilled across the clearing, Nisrine turned again toward Seren. He met her gaze, eyes dark with memory, with questions neither of them had time to ask. But he gave a single nod, slow and sure.

We're here.

She returned it, the edge of her fingers brushing his once more as she passed. Not quite a promise. But not nothing, either.

Together, they stepped forward, the pulse of the broken gate at their backs, and the uncertain road ahead.

Chapter 22

A long row of nobles and advisors lined either side of the central dais where King Lonan presided, crowned in gold, wrapped in silence. He had not spoken for nearly an hour. The High Court of Constalatia sat in strained stillness, the obsidian-pillared hall cloaked in flickering firelight.

The nobles squirmed, their whispered concerns growing bolder: whispers of rebellion, a growing unrest in the common districts. But Lonan did not answer. He watched the flickering sconces along the walls as though reading prophecy in their flames.

Suddenly, the fire nearest him extinguished with a sharp hiss. Then another. A draft swept through the hall, curling down the center aisle like smoke on the tide of some unseen shift.

The king's hand gripped the carved armrest of his throne. Then he felt it.

A crack in the realm. A sharp fracture in the foundation of the world as he had shaped it. Like something snapping inside his very bones.

He stood.

The council chamber fell silent.

Eyes turned to him as the flame behind the throne flared unnaturally high, then twisted sideways, pulled by an unseen current. The air buzzed with tension, raw, ancient, and wrong.

One of the spellcasters at the far end of the room gasped and fell to their knees. "The gate," she whispered, hands trembling. "Something's happened to the gate."

"It's been shattered," Lonan said, voice low and dangerous, resounding like thunder. His gaze was distant. His irises shimmered with violet, pulsing in time with something undetectable.

Another sconce went dark. Panic rippled through the court like lightning over water.

Gasps rang out. One noble stepped back as if the floor had burned him. Another dropped his quill in the sudden nervousness. The court froze, waiting, dreading what would come next.

King Lonan's magic flared around him in a ring of violet fire. The torches guttered violently. His expression was cold, but his voice, when it came, was anything but.

"Seal the corridors. Double the inner guard. No one leaves the palace without my approval." He turned sharply to Captain Veyric, who had just entered the hall. "Mobilize the Shadow Claws. All of them. If the gate is shattered, it means she's opened a path for more than just her allies."

"But Your Majesty," Veyric began, already sweating beneath his armor, "we don't yet know where she..."

"*You will find her.*" Lonan's voice cracked like a whip, sending a tremor through the walls. "Nisrine has betrayed her realm, her people, and her birthright. She is no longer to be treated as royalty. Bring her back. Bound and unconscious if necessary."

"And if she resists?" asked another noble, trembling.

Lonan's smile was sharp and terrifying. "Then remind her what fear feels like."

Murmurs swept the court like dry leaves. Fear. Yes. That, they understood. That, they had been raised on, even if they'd convinced themselves it was respect.

Lonan turned to his court scribe, his voice lower but no less lethal. "Send ravens to the Court of Embers and the Drowned Vale. Tell them the girl has destabilized the boundary and risked the old magic returning. Let them feel the threat. Let them beg me for protection."

The scribe's ink splattered across the parchment from his trembling hands.

Without another word, Lonan strode from the room, his cloak of shadows trailing like a spill of night. The court remained silent until the echo of his boots vanished entirely.

Though the stone walls of the king's chambers dulled the wind, an unnatural current still hissed through the cracks. Lonan stood at the wide glass window, watching as the gilded rooftops of the Fae capital sank into shadow beneath a roiling sky.

Turning from the window, he traced his hand along the mirror beside the hearth. Its surface shivered with ancient magic. Not a looking glass. No. A conduit. A spyglass into things just out of reach, yet pliable to his will, given time.

His daughter.

No. Not his. Not anymore.

Cherith's.

Lonan turned sharply from the mirror, pacing the edge of the room. His boots clicked against the obsidian inlaid floor. Frost breath escaped between clenched teeth in the unnaturally cold air of the chamber.

"She was never meant to survive in that world," he muttered. "She was meant to suffer it, to learn its cruelty and crawl back."

But Nisrine had not crawled. She had stood. And shattered everything.

He moved to the table at the center of the chamber where old documents lay, aged by time and sealed with the broken wax of ancient courts. Some bore Cherith's script, soft curves, graceful flourishes, and Lonan hated how even now, her hand unsettled him.

On Fallen Wings

Their marriage had never been his choice. She was the daughter of a nobleman whose fortunes were faltering. A man cunning enough to secure an audience with the king, Lonan's father, and bargain his way into power. Whatever promises or threats had passed between them, it ended with Cherith bound to Lonan by decree, not desire. At the time, he'd expected a quiet, dutiful wife.

Instead, she had been more brilliant than he expected, more dangerous than any court had guessed.

And Nisrine had become the same.

He ran a fingertip over one of the remaining pages: scrawled protections, old diagrams of what lay beneath the stone circles. The truth of it was simple and infuriating. Cherith had *planned* for this. Hidden spells and backdoors inside old magic. Planted them like seeds, waiting for someone, *her daughter*, to bloom into the key.

Lonan slammed his fist against the table. Papers flew. A lone rune-bone rolled and bounced with a muted clatter to the floor.

He didn't retrieve it right away.

Instead, he stared down at the flames licking low in the hearth. Purple and black, tinged with silver. A conjuring fire fed by no ordinary wood. He whispered a spell under his breath, ancient and cruel, and the fire surged, revealing a vision in the mirror: *Nisrine surrounded by rebels.* One of them, half-Fae by the look of him, stood far too close.

Corvan.

The name rose like bile in Lonan's throat.

He knew that face. Knew the sharpness of the jawline, the grey eyes threaded with silver. Corvan bore the face of his father. A Fae traitor who had once dared to take a human mate. A soldier-turned-renegade, who vanished not long after marrying the human. Lonan had seen to it. Quietly. Thoroughly.

Lonan thought the bloodline had ended with him. But here the boy was. Grown, breathing, standing too near to Nisrine like fate had rewritten itself. Like something buried had clawed its way back to the service.

His eyes narrowed as he muttered, "Of course it would be Calreth's offspring. Of all the ghosts..."

He picked up the rune-bone at last, weighing it in his hand. Not just a relic. A failsafe. A leash.

There were other magics older than tethers. Older than gates. Older than choice.

He turned to the sealed door behind the hearth. Few knew it existed. Fewer still dared enter.

But now? Now it was time.

He whispered, "Orriven," and the stone door unlatched with a soft hiss.

Inside, the chamber pulsed with cold light. Runes lined the walls. Sigils of control, domination, and memory. And in its center: a pool of still black water, reflecting nothing.

He stepped into the room and stood at its edge.

"If she will not return to me willingly," Lonan said softly, "then I will call her back in the only language the old magic understands."

The pool shivered.

Lonan closed his eyes, drawing upon the dark thread of the tether that remained. The first one, the one no one but he and

Cherith had ever fully understood. The one hidden in Nisrine's blood.

"She has broken the gate," he said to the magic. "Now I break the silence."

And somewhere across the worlds, something ancient stirred.

Chapter 23

They found an abandoned chapel in the hollow that offered little in the way of comfort, but at least it kept the rain off their heads. Moss crept in through the cracks in the stone floor, and part of the roof sagged where a tree branch had smashed through the far side years ago. But the walls still held, ancient stone laced with vines, thick enough to keep out wind and sight. For now, it was enough.

Nisrine stood near what might once have been an altar, fingers brushing the edge of the weathered stone. The cold bit through her skin, but she barely noticed. Around her, low voices murmured. Reports from the scouts who had circled back to watch the gate. They spoke of strange echoes, of lights in the trees that vanished when approached. The threads of magic left behind from the shattered gate were like spider silk. Barely visible and endlessly shifting. Seren had called it "residue." Corvan called it "wounded magic."dd

"It's closing slower than I thought," Corvan murmured, stepping beside her.

She turned toward him, and her brow furrowed. "That's good, isn't it?"

He shook his head once. "No. It means the rupture is unstable. If anything else comes through, Fae, beast, or worse, we won't know until it's breathing down our necks."

Her lips pressed together, a faint crease forming between her brows. She didn't say what she was thinking. That part of her wished something *would* come through. *Or someone else. Someone like my mother.*

But she didn't say it. Instead, her gaze slid across the room, drawn not to Corvan but to Seren.

He stood near the opposite wall, speaking quietly with Olesia and Thalen, his shoulders tense beneath his armor. The torchlight cast warm shadows over his face, softening the edges she knew too well. His brows tightened, head bent slightly in thought. Always thinking ahead. Always watching.

Then his eyes lifted and found hers. The world muted around them. Just a look. Nothing more. But it held emotions they hadn't said since stepping through that gate. Regret. Relief. Worry. The impossible weight of having found one another again only to keep moving forward into an unknown darkness.

He didn't smile. But his expression shifted, barely. Just enough to soften. Just enough to steady her.

And then, he stepped toward her. Quietly. Purposefully. She didn't look away.

He stopped just shy of touching her, close enough that she could feel the warmth radiating from him, his breath mingling with hers in the cold, still air.

"You should rest," he said softly, voice lower than before. Just for her. "You burned through more power than you realize. Your hands are still shaking."

She glanced down. He was right. Her fingers trembled slightly against the stone. "I'm fine," she said, too quickly. "It'll pass."

He didn't argue.

But his hand rose. Tentative, unsure. And for a heartbeat, it hovered above hers. Then, slowly, he let his fingers brush hers. Just the edge. A breath of contact.

Her breath caught.

"I didn't know if I'd ever see you again," he said, barely audible. "When the gate shattered, I thought… I thought we were too late."

"I know. Me too," she whispered.

Another heartbeat.

Then came a *bang,* sharp and jarring.

The heavy wooden door crashed open, the sound echoing through the stone like a thunderclap. Everyone jumped. Steel rang as blades were drawn in a blur, feet shifting, instincts crackling to life.

Seren's sword was in hand before the echo faded. He stepped in front of Nisrine without thinking, body shield raised, expression carved from stone.

"Dade!" The name broke from Nisrine's lips before she realized it. Relief bloomed sharp and sudden in her chest.

There he stood in the doorway, Dade. Soaked, panting, sleeve torn and spattered with something dark. No smirk. No sarcasm. Just raw, wild exhaustion.

Seren's voice cut through the tension like a blade. "Who is this?"

"A friend," Nisrine said quickly.

Seren didn't lower his sword. But he stepped back. Just enough to let her through.

Just enough to say: *I trust you.*

"She's gone," he rasped.

Nisrine froze. "What?"

"Elaila," Dade said, voice cracking with fury. "She was watching the ridge like we planned. Then two of King Lonan's males, maybe three, ambushed her. Definitely not human. Tracked her down like dogs. I... I tried, but she..."

He staggered forward, soaked to the bone, blood and rain smeared across his cheek. His breath hitched. "They took her, Nisrine!"

For a heartbeat, no one moved. The only sound was the steady tap of rain through the broken roof, each drop landing like a countdown.

Seren stepped to her side, close enough that she could feel the heat of him in the cold air. His hand settled lightly on her shoulder, grounding her. Not stopping her, never that, but offering his silent question: *Are you steady?*

Her pulse hammered in her throat. She nodded once.

Then she stepped forward, raising her hands slowly. Her voice was calm but firm.

"Weapons down, everyone. This is my friend, Dade. His companion, and my friend, has been taken. They saved me from the guards before I found Corvan."

The group obeyed, tension easing just slightly, but not entirely. Dade leaned against the wall, drenched and shaking. "They took her to the lowlands."

Mirell was the first to speak. "You're sure she was alive?"

Dade nodded once, his face expression hardening. "Alive, yes. Conscious... probably not. She fought like hell. One of them was dragging her. The others were bleeding."

Seren straightened, drawing in a sharp breath. "Where are the lowlands?"

"Past the ash grove, near the broken aqueduct. I didn't follow too closely. They would've seen me. I ran towards Nisrine's scent. Fast as I could."

Seren looked at Nisrine with an unspoken question on his face.

Dade gave a humorless smile that didn't reach his eyes. "And before anyone asks how I tracked her scent across half the forest... We're vampires."

A few in the group stiffened.

Nisrine added, "And we can't leave her."

"No one said we would," Seren said.

He turned his head slightly, his gaze brushing against hers. At that moment, he didn't look like a commander. Just a male caught between duty and something far more personal. His fingers flexed at his side like he was trying not to reach for her again.

On Fallen Wings

Corvan crossed the room, his voice cutting through the rising urgency. "If they've taken her, they'll hold her for information. Or worse, use her as bait."

"She *fought* for me," Nisrine said, teeth clenched. "I'm not leaving her in their hands."

Dade sank further against the wall. "We've got a window. Maybe a day before they vanish underground or deliver her to someone who won't hesitate to rip her mind apart. Elaila's strong, but she's not invincible."

Aeron looked at Seren. "We'll need two groups. One to intercept, one to fall back and cover retreat."

"I'll lead the intercept," Seren said immediately.

"I'm going," Nisrine said, stepping in before he could assign her anywhere else. Her tone was unwavering. "She wouldn't be in this mess if it weren't for me."

"Nisrine," Corvan started.

"She's part of this," she said, turning her eyes to him. "So am I."

Corvan hesitated, but it was Seren who answered.

He didn't argue. Didn't try to talk her down. He just nodded once. That same quiet acceptance he'd always offered her, even when it broke every rule he was supposed to follow.

"Then we leave in ten," he said. "Light gear. No fire. No magic flares until we find her."

Dade straightened, pushing off the wall, a flicker of his old fire returning. "She'll kill me for letting them take her, you know."

"Good," Nisrine said, brushing past him. "Let's make sure she gets the chance."

She moved quickly toward the back of the large room to gather her things, but Seren caught her hand gently as she passed.

Their eyes met in the half-light.

"I'll stay close," he murmured, not as a promise, but as a vow. "No matter what we find out there."

The words settled between them, heavy as iron, soft as breath.

"I know," she whispered.

And for a single heartbeat, their fingers stayed locked. Just long enough to remember what they were risking. Just long enough to say: *I'm still here.*

Then she pulled away.

And they moved.

Together.

Twilight dripped through the branches like blood through gauze, dim and heavy. The group moved in silence, urgency pressing them forward along the narrow ridge trail. Seren led with his blade drawn. Dade flanked the rear, his dark coat fluttering with every motion. Olesia and Corvan kept close to Nisrine, casting guarded glances toward every shifting shadow.

They were tracking Elaila's captors, fast-moving and highly trained Fae of the king. But the deeper they moved into the trees, the more the world began to... bend.

At first, it was subtle.

A hush that wasn't natural. The wind died. The birds and insects fell silent.

Then, the pressure came. Slow and coiling, like snakes constricting around their heads.

Nisrine felt it first. A chill not of weather, but of something older. Something watching. Her fingers brushed the hilt at her hip, but it was her breath she steadied. A flicker of movement ahead made Seren raise his fist, halting the group.

They rounded a bend slowly, and the forest simply stopped.

The trees there were dead things, hollow and blackened like they'd burned from the inside out. The ground cracked beneath their steps, the air dry with silence. And at the clearing's center stood a figure cloaked in shifting shadow, faceless and wrong, as if its shape was borrowed and barely held together.

They froze.

Weapons were raised. Spells shimmered at the ready.

Seren moved slightly to his right, instinctively shielding Nisrine's path with his body. His stance never faltered, but she saw it. The quick flick of his gaze to her, the tension in his grip that spoke of more than duty.

The figure drifted forward, not walking, but gliding. Its joints bent in ways that defied anatomy, like it had learned movement from a nightmare.

The forest behind them sealed itself shut.

"What is that?" Seren muttered under his breath, angling his sword in front of her now.

"A force that should have stayed buried," Corvan said grimly, stepping protectively to Nisrine's other side. "It shouldn't be awake."

The shadow paused, tilting its head as if studying them. No. *Studying her.*

"You've woken us from our long slumber, child," it rasped.

The voice came from nowhere. From *everywhere.* It echoed not just in their ears, but in their bones. The pressure intensified. Even the magic around them shrank back, recoiling from the presence like prey sensing a predator.

"What is it talking about?" Olesia whispered.

Nisrine didn't take her eyes off the figure. "I think it's from the other side of the barrier," she said quietly. "Something that was sealed away when the Fae were."

"Fantastic," Dade muttered. "Ancient forest demon. That's what we needed today."

Nisrine stepped forward, only to feel Seren's fingers graze her wrist. Just enough to make her pause. His eyes locked with hers, quiet but intense. *You don't have to do this alone.*

She offered him the smallest nod, her hand brushing over his as she passed. *I know. But I'm still going.*

She faced the figure. "Who are you? Why are you here?"

The creature seemed to shudder with amusement. "You broke the seal. You tore the veil. We are The Eidolon, buried and forgotten in the dark so your kind could rule in the light. Now we return."

And then it raised its arm.

A wave of black energy howled toward them like a tidal wind.

Nisrine's magic flared before she could think, silver and gold crashing upward into a shield. She held it, though it tore through her like fire, rattling her bones and sending her to one knee. Still, she held.

"You are naive, Princess," the shadow hissed, dripping with disdain, "You are the *key* to your people's undoing. You are the crack through which the dark will flood. The Fae are *not* meant to be free. You were sealed away for a reason. We, the ones who were forgotten, are the rightful rulers. The Fae are nothing. And now, you've unleashed us."

Tendrils of darkness erupted from the soil, spiraling toward her.

Seren struck one aside with a clean slash, his blade humming with wardlight. "Back off!" he growled.

Corvan grabbed her arm, his voice sharp. "Don't let it in. Don't let it take root."

But Nisrine could barely hear them. Her magic was splitting at the seams. Her thoughts frayed, fear clawing its way into her ribs.

The balance was tipping. Her mind reeled. And then she heard her mother's voice.

"The magic is not meant to be controlled. It is meant to be balanced. Creation and destruction, light and shadow. Accept both and shape the world, not break it."

She gasped, her body jolting as she dropped to both knees, clutching at whoever was closest.

Her grip tightened on Corvan's arm. Then, blindly, she reached for Seren.

He was there in an instant.

Their hands met, her fingers trembling, his calloused palm grounding her. He didn't speak. He didn't need to. His presence said it all.

195

I'm here. I believe in you.

Her breath shuddered out. She closed her eyes. And let go.

No more fighting the dark. No more clinging to the light. She let them spiral together, twining, fusing, braiding into something whole. Not peace. Not chaos. But power.

It surged through her, too vast for her body to contain. With a thunderous crack, the clearing erupted. Light and shadow spun into a cyclone that hurled everyone backward. Corvan and Seren were ripped from her grasp as if they'd never been there at all.

The shadow reeled, shrieking as its form wavered, flickering violently.

"You... you carry *both* halves," it spat.

Nisrine rose to her feet, steady and radiant, her voice fierce. "I carry the whole."

She thrust both hands forward. The balanced magic surged outward like a spear of lightning and darkness punching through the Eidolon's chest. The figure howled, unraveling into mist.

Before it vanished completely, its voice returned, quieter now, more like a whisper beneath the skin: *"This is only the beginning, Princess. The darkness cannot be contained forever. We will rise again."*

The silence left behind was deafening.

Nisrine dropped to her knees again, breath ragged.

Corvan, still sprawled where he'd landed, reached toward her but couldn't close the distance.

Seren was already moving, pushing himself upright, sprinting the last steps, and dropping to his knees beside her. Wordlessly, his hands curled around hers like a lifeline.

"You're alright," he murmured, so quietly no one else could hear. His forehead nearly touched hers. "You're alright," he repeated.

"I almost lost it," she whispered back. "I... I heard her, Seren."

"I know." He brushed her cheek with his thumb.

The others slowly regrouped, shaken but intact.

Seren stood, helping her to her feet, but never let go of her hand. Not even when he turned to the others and said, "We need to move. If *that* came through, other *things* will follow."

Olesia crouched beside the scorched earth. "The gate didn't just crack the barrier. It cracked the prison."

Nisrine drew a deep breath. Her limbs trembled, but she stood tall. "Then we find Elaila. We don't stop."

No one argued. Not even Corvan.

And as they stepped into the dark forest again, Nisrine felt Seren's fingers linger at the small of her back, just a whisper of contact.

I'm with you. Whatever comes next.

She didn't say anything. But she didn't need to.

She walked forward. And he followed.

Chapter 24

The forest slowly began to breathe again.

Where silence had strangled every branch, now wind stirred. Timid at first, then stronger. Leaves rustled like whispers daring to speak. A bird cried in the distance. The world was waking up, one sound at a time, unsure if it was safe to return.

Nisrine stood in the center of the clearing, her breath shallow. Her hands twitched at her sides, still faintly glowing from the magic she had unleashed. It coiled in her veins like a storm subdued but not spent.

No one spoke. Not yet.

Seren moved first.

His boots crunched softly through the blackened underbrush. He didn't look at her. He looked at Corvan, tension carved into his features "What the hell was that thing?"

Corvan straightened slowly, brushing ash from his coat. His voice rasped, rough with dread. "An Eidolon... Something ancient. Something that was never meant to be free again."

Olesia stepped closer, eyes narrowed. "Ancient I understand. But what is it?"

Corvan's gaze flicked to her, then to the scorched earth. "A shadow of something that lived before the first seal. Older than the barrier and any courts." His tone darkened. "They say it feeds on more than just flesh. On the self. It unravels you, thread by thread, until there's nothing left to remember you were ever alive."

Nisrine's stomach knotted. "How do you know that?"

"I've heard fragments," Corvan admitted. "Heard whispers from those old enough to remember... but I've never seen one. Not until tonight. And I'd prefer not to ever again." He looked directly at Nisrine then, his face tight with concern. "You could've been killed."

"I know," Nisrine whispered. "But it would've followed us. Or worse. I couldn't let it."

Aeron cursed softly and swept the perimeter, sword still drawn. "We're not ready for things like that. That wasn't just horrifying... it was...blasphemous."

"We weren't ready for any of this," Seren said. He turned and gestured toward the center of the clearing, where the shadow had stood moments before. "But here we are. We don't dare back out now."

Nisrine met his gaze, and something passed between them. Exhaustion, yes, but also a quiet understanding. He hadn't stopped her. He'd trusted her.

Corvan spoke again, his tone grim. "More will come. That confirms the gate didn't only let you through."

A heavy silence fell, like a held breath.

Nisrine's limbs ached with the effort it had taken to defeat the dark figure, but there was no time to rest. Elaila was still in danger. Every second wasted could cost her everything.

They kept moving forward.

Corvan led the way now, his senses sharp. Behind him moved Seren, silent but watchful, his sword still drawn. Dade walked a few paces behind them, his usual sarcastic grin replaced by a taut, haunted look.

"She's still alive," he said, his voice tight. "Elaila. I can feel her, barely. They've done something to her. Her heartbeat is dim, but it's there."

Nisrine straightened. The ache in her limbs didn't matter anymore. "Which way?"

Corvan crouched low, fingers brushing the ground. "The trail's fresh. No effort to hide it. They weren't worried about being followed."

"They should be," Seren muttered, already moving.

On Fallen Wings

They followed the trail into the deepening woods, a winding path of snapped branches and scattered drops of blood. Nisrine's heart pounded harder with each step.

Nisrine stopped suddenly and bent down. She brushed a hand over the dirt where something glinted faintly. A broken pin from Elaila's cloak. Blood coated it.

"She didn't go easy," Nisrine said quietly.

"She never does," Dade murmured. But his voice broke at the edges.

They emerged near the husk of an old aqueduct, ivy draped like burial shrouds over its collapsing frame. The stones leached cold, and shadows pooled unnaturally in the corners.

"They're here," Corvan said, his voice sharper now.

Nisrine nodded.

Seren signaled with two fingers, split and surround.

Aeron, Olesia, and Thalen vanished into the trees, looping around the left flank, silent as wraiths. Dade, tense as wire, stayed behind Nisrine and Seren as they approached the front.

And then they saw her.

Elaila was bound to an iron spike driven into the ground, her arms outstretched. Silver-black cuffs shimmered with sickly runes, biting into her wrists. Her face was pale, too pale, and her head hung low. But her chest rose and fell.

Alive. Barely.

Two Fae males lingered nearby. One leaned against a broken pillar, bored. The other paced with a curved blade, watching her like a wolf circling a wounded deer.

Dade froze. His eyes widened as panic coiled in his chest. His hand curled around the hilt of his dagger, knuckles

201

white. "They're draining her," Dade hissed. "Collecting her blood. Using it to strengthen whatever spellwork Lonan has planned."

Something inside Nisrine snapped. She stepped into the open, and the air seemed to twist around her, glowing threads of magic snaking along her fingertips. She lifted her voice, crisp and resonant, echoing off the stones: "Let her go."

The pacing male turned, startled, but then his mouth curled into a smirk. "Princess. We figured you'd come." It was the same guard who chased her from Elaila and Dade's camp.

The other drew his weapon, silent, but deadly fast.

Seren surged forward with a growl, intercepting the blade before it could swing, steel clashing with steel in a blinding flash.

Olesia's spell shot in from the trees, white fire blinding the first guard as Corvan rushed in behind him, blade low and fast.

Dade was already running, sliding to his knees beside Elaila. "I've got you; I've got you," he murmured, fingers shaking as he began to trace the markings that bound her.

Nisrine felt the ward around Elaila begin to unravel. She stepped forward, palms glowing with twin lights of silver and shadow, and pressed her hands to the cuffs. The bindings split with a violent snap. Elaila cried out. Not the hollow echo of the ward, but her own voice at last. Fierce. Living. Alive.

Elaila's eyes opened. She ripped one hand free and slammed it onto the earth. The shadows around them recoiled like smoke, and the remnants of the ward shattered in a ripple of power. "That's my girl," Dade breathed through his smile, catching her as she sagged against him.

The guard lunged, but Corvan was faster. His blade punched clean through the Fae's chest. The body fell hard and didn't move again.

Corvan scanned the perimeter as he panted. "Clear," he barked.

Nisrine dropped to her knees beside Elaila. Her magic was flickering at her fingertips again, instinctive and raw, but Elaila no longer needed it. She was breathing. Awake. Alive.

"You came for me," Elaila rasped.

Nisrine smiled, though her eyes shimmered with tears. "Of course we did. You were there for me first, and that means you're family. One of us."

Seren stood over them, breathing hard, blood streaked down his sword arm. He looked at Nisrine. Not the princess, not the wielder of strange magic, but her. Just her.

And for the briefest moment, the fear faded.

Chapter 25

He was just a boy of ten, called a princeling by the older Fae of the court. A term spoken with equal parts fondness and dismissal.

The sky had been overcast the day of the sealing, the ground sodden with stormwater. The grove where they gathered was a place no longer found on any map, a place the earth itself tried to forget.

He remembered how the mud soaked his boot, how the scent of wet ash clung to everything. He remembered the circle. Stones, half-buried in the dirt lined with salt and sigils carved deep, magic pulsing with fear.

And he remembered her.

Cherith, still young then, stood tall at her mother's side, her hands bare, her hair wind-snatched and wild. She looked like fury itself, radiant and unflinching. She hadn't glanced back at him, but he'd watched her.

The ritual circle glowed. Thirteen Fae had formed the perimeter, arms raised, their pointed ears bleeding with the strain of the invocation.

And in the center of the circle, *they* writhed.

The Eidolon.

Not beasts, not spirits. Something worse. They were raw will, ancient and hungry, pressed into the shape of nightmares. One moment they looked like shadow-born giants, the next like nothing at all. Just *absence*.

They weren't demons, not in the way stories called them. They had once been something like the Fae. Twisted now, altered by power they didn't understand. Shadows with bones, with memories, with rage. The moment the first one was brought forward, bound in shackles of iron, runestone, and salt, his stomach turned. Not from the horror. From the recognition. Its face was barely a face, but its voice, when it laughed, sounded like someone once known.

The ritual began to hum.

And then, chaos.

One of the circle mages collapsed. Blood burst from her nose and her mouth. The seal began to falter. The ground cracked.

He didn't mean to get closer, but his feet moved, as if something pulled him down to the circle. An invisible obstacle. He fell.

His head struck a stone, and the blood came. It poured into his eyes, hot and stinging. When he blinked, the world shimmered red. Blurred and trembling.

He looked up, and one of the creatures looked back.

It *saw* him.

Not a threat. Not a hero.

Just a boy. But a boy with something wild and broken in him.

"You would never seal us," it whispered, though no one else heard. *"You want to know what we know."*

He did.

Even then, though he didn't yet understand it. The world the elders had made, so careful, so bound in rules, felt wrong, brittle and fearful. He didn't want peace. He wanted the *truth*. He wanted power enough to never be sent away. Never be left behind.

The creature laughed.

"You will remember this. And so will we."

One by one, the Eidolon were banished. Pushed through an arch of light laced with barbed magic, sealed into a prison between worlds. Not killed. Just caged. To be forgotten.

But not by him.

Not by the boy with blood in his eyes, who watched the seals close like doors that might never open again. Not by the boy who heard the creature's voice that would follow him into his dreams.

And not by Cherith, who turned once to look at him and saw what he couldn't yet name in himself.

Pity. Or warning.

And as the final seal locked into place, the twelve remaining Fae collapsed, dying to forge it, he screamed.

Not for the fallen. Not for the sealed-away horrors.

But because something precious had been stolen from him: a *possibility*.

And he never forgave the world for taking it.

The shattered remnants of the barrier still shimmered in the sky behind him, like the cracked edge of a mirror that no longer reflected light.

King Lonan stepped through the veil, his cloak of midnight velvet swirling around his legs as he entered the human world for the first time in many years. The land felt thinner here, too fragile to hold true power, but the scent of ancient magic still hung in the air, faint and burned around the edges. It called to him.

He didn't come alone. A cadre of loyal guards flanked him. The Shadow Claws were the finest of the King's elite, their armor enchanted, their eyes dead to doubt. Lonan barely spared them a glance. His gaze was fixed on the forest ahead, specifically, the place where the world had bent. Where something had passed through and never fully closed behind it.

A place touched by the Forgotten.

He stepped into the clearing slowly. The trees were wrong here. Twisted, blackened, their roots curled like claws through the earth. The air buzzed faintly, as if some great presence had only just vacated the space. Not long ago, something had been summoned, or awakened.

And it had tasted freedom.

One of the guards shifted nervously behind him. "Sire… this place isn't natural."

"No," Lonan said. "It's better."

With a single gesture, he dismissed them. "Stay back. Whatever lingers here does not tolerate fear."

They obeyed without hesitation.

Lonan knelt at the heart of the clearing. He placed one palm against the scorched ground, letting the ash swirl around his fingers, and whispered an incantation to call them forward. "Atrum. Veni!"

The air split.

A ripple moved through the clearing, as though the trees had inhaled. Then, nothing.

He closed his eyes and opened his mind. Not to the clean magic of the court, not to the rigid language of balance and boundaries. But to the old voice. The one that whispered beneath the skin of the world. It was wild. Hungry. Beautiful. Something shifted. The shadows grew longer.

Then it came.

Not in form, but in presence. A cold that pressed into the hollows of their bones. The trees bent inward. The ground pulsed.

Lonan remained unshaken.

A voice slid through the dark. *"You are not the one who freed us."*

"No," he said. "But I know who did. And I seek what she woke."

Silence. Then, *"Why?"*

"Because I am done with waiting. With balance. I know what sleeps beneath the old seals. I know what was sacrificed to keep the realms apart. And I know it was a mistake."

A soft, serpentine whisper curled through the air. *"You speak as those did. Before the first seal. You speak like one who would end the world to remake it."*

"I would burn it to the ground," Lonan said calmly, a cruel smile forming, "if it meant building something stronger from the ash."

The darkness shifted. A shape began to form between the trees, not flesh, but suggestion. A towering silhouette of moving shadow, joints bending in directions they weren't meant to, tendrils of darkness flickering with every motion, echoing the Eidolon Nisrine had faced.

"Your kind locked us away. Buried us in silence."

"And now," Lonan murmured, "I'm inviting you."

Another breath.

"You are not like the girl. She carries light and shadow. You are only void."

A savage smile curled on Lonan's lips. "Then perhaps we understand each other."

It moved closer. The guards behind him stumbled, one of them falling to his knees as the pressure mounted. Lonan did not turn. His eyes were fixed on the abyss that took shape before him.

"What do you want, King of the dying court?"

"To make a bargain."

The wind shifted. The forest seemed to listen.

"What will you offer?"

Lonan held out his hand. Not as a gesture of peace, but of invitation. "A path back. A way for your kind to thrive in this world again. Not by fracture, but by force."

The Eidolon paused.

Then, with a voice like broken stone, "And what do you seek in return?"

"Your strength. Your knowledge. Your hunger." His voice dropped. "I will break her. I will drag my daughter from the world and remind her who she was born to be. She is the key. And she will either kneel, or I will use her magic to open every door she tries to close."

"We remember you now. The boy with blood in his eyes. The one who watched the sealing. The one who wanted it undone."

Lonan smiled. "Then you know I speak true."

Silence again, heavy and waiting.

Then the creature lowered itself, whispering with something like reverence, like a promise, "Very well. The pact has begun."

Lonan's hand clenched. A searing heat bloomed across his palm. The mark was a brutal smear of darkness, like inked blood burning from within, curling and twisting with unnatural life. Each pulse of heat made it glow, as if the last embers of a dying star were trapped just beneath his skin.

The Eidolon vanished into the trees, but its voice lingered, curling through the clearing like smoke. *"You will not survive what you summon."*

Lonan turned, his eyes gleaming with a darkness deeper than shadow. "I will survive. I will rise from the fire and let the world burn behind me."

And as he walked from the clearing, the forest behind him began to rot, leaves curling inward, bark cracking, roots blackening as something old and long-buried stirred awake.

The forest in her dream was wrong.

It stretched on forever, but the trees had no leaves, only blackened, skeletal limbs scratching at a blood-red sky. The ground throbbed beneath her bare feet, pulsing like a heartbeat. In the distance, something old and monstrous stirred. A low groan echoing through the void between the trees. Shadows twisted unnaturally at the corners of her vision.

Then came the voice.

Not loud. Not shouted. Just *present,* deep and honey-dark, as if whispered directly into her bones.

"You are my blood. You cannot outrun me."

Nisrine turned. Shadows swirled, but no figure came into view. Only a burning mark in the air like a seal scorched into reality itself, hovering just inches from her chest. It pulsed once… and then shattered like glass. King Lonan's face revealed itself in the shattered pieces.

She gasped and bolted upright.

The tent's canvas rustled in the quiet night. Her chest heaved. A cold sweat clung to her skin.

Dade was already there crouching beside her bedroll. He didn't speak at first, just watched her with a stillness that said he'd been nearby while she tossed and turned.

"You're alright," he said softly. "You're safe."

She shook her head. "No. It was him. My father. I heard him, *felt* him. He's… he's made a pact. It's starting."

Dade's eyes flicked to the corner of the tent, his expression darkening. "Did you see what he's bound to?"

"The forest around me was wrong. Dead." Her voice cracked. "It felt like the end of everything… the Eidolon."

Dade reached over and gently handed her a water flask. "Drink."

Her fingers trembled around the metal as she drank.

"You're not crazy," he said after a beat. "I've felt something, too. Like the air's stretched too thin. Something moving underneath it."

She glanced at him. "You don't sleep. You would know."

"Yeah." He offered a small, tired smile. "Perks of being undead."

Nisrine tried to smile back, but her lips barely moved.

Dade's voice lowered. "Whatever he sent you… It rattled you pretty hard. You don't have to handle that alone."

She met his gaze and gave a small, grateful nod.

Dade smirked, "Creepy forest? Ominous family drama? Handsome vampire hero? Check, check, and check."

Nisrine laughed, and the tightness in her chest eased just a little.

Chapter 26

The world was changing.

At first, it was only in ways most would miss, a strange shimmer along the edges of lakes, trees that leaned toward sounds, wind that carried scents from places it shouldn't. But Nisrine felt it in her skin, in the marrow of her bones. Magic was stirring. Not just Fae magic, but the deep, old magic that once wove both realms together before the divide.

It had begun the moment the gate shattered. The veil between the worlds was no longer whole.

Where the human realm ended, the Fae bled in, twisting the land until it was neither one nor the other.

And something else came with it.

Some nights as they walked to a new village to see how many allies they could gather, they saw strange silhouettes between the trees. Creatures too thin, too tall, with too many eyes, or none at all.

"They're slipping through," Corvan said one night, voice low, eyes narrowed to the shadows beyond. "Not just the Fae. The others. The ones the seal held back."

Nisrine didn't answer. He saw the tension in her jaw, the way her fingers curled slightly toward her side as though they still remembered the shape of the sword.

Every day, more of the wildness returned. Old ruins flickered into view that had been hidden for generations. Rivers carved new paths through ancient valleys. The constellations themselves began to shift, stars no longer followed the patterns she had memorized as a child. Elaila said the ley lines had cracked. Dade said the world was starting to remember itself, and it didn't like what it saw.

But Nisrine didn't falter. She couldn't.

While others fled, she walked into it, gathering those who still held fast to the old oaths.

The mountain swallowed them in shadow, its stone corridors narrowing like the throat of some ancient beast. Frost clung to the walls, and every breath turned to mist, stolen from their lungs by the cold. Their footsteps echoed, an intruder's rhythm in a place that had forgotten warmth.

On Fallen Wings

In the high council chamber, the air thickened. Ghostlights hovered in wide glass bowls suspended from thin chains, their pale blue glow rippling across carved pillars and painting the faces of the gathered nobles like shades of the dead. No laughter. No whispers. Only the steady weight of a hundred eyes measuring her.

An old woman rose at last, her cloak of white wolf fur whispering across the floor. With each step, the silver head of her cane struck like a slow heartbeat in the silence. Deep creases carved her face, yet her eyes remained clear, hard as river ice. She leaned on the cane, letting the question drop like a blade: "Your father's court banished us. What do you offer to make us forget?"

Nisrine stepped forward, and the ghostlights flared brighter, as though drawn by her presence. For a moment, her reflection burned in the old woman's gaze, her eyes alive with fire no exile could quench. "Forget nothing," she said, voice carrying into every shadowed corner of the room. "Fight beside me, and the world that exiled you will answer for what it's done."

A ripple passed through the chamber, not applause but the low murmurs of old grudges stirring awake.

Some nobles leaned forward, their eyes sharp with hunger for vengeance. Others scoffed under their breath, wolf-fur and bone ornaments shifting with the movement.

The old woman's cane tapped once, silencing the murmurs. Her mouth curved into something that was not quite a smile. "Brazen words, child of Lonan. Let us see if they are more than fire on your tongue."

She inclined her head the slightest fraction, and as she did, the other nobles followed. A ripple of reluctant acknowledgement passing through the chamber. The air shifted; the pact was real, and Nistine felt the ground steady beneath her feet.

They continued on. Court after court weaving alliances like threads in a tapestry. Old allies who had remained hidden for years, druids, tree-singers, stonewalkers, came out of hiding to stand at her side. At each gathering, Nisrine stood before them with her chin lifted, voice calm but edged with a steel they had never heard before.

"You remember the stories of the world before the gates," she told them. "You remember what we were, what we lost. If we stand divided, Lonan will break us piece by piece. If we stand together, we will remind him that we do not bow, we rise."

She paused, letting the silence settle.

"I do not promise you safety," she continued, her words clear, "but I promise you a chance to fight for the future our ancestors dreamed of. A future where no king steals our choices or our lives out of fear."

Some nodded, grimly resolute. Others looked away, fear clouding their faces.

"I will stand with you," she said, letting the fire in her heart burn through every word. "Not above you. With you. As your shield, as your blade, as your sister. If you will have me."

It was enough for some.

Some joined because they believed in her. Some, because they remembered Queen Cherith. And some, because they saw the tide rising and knew that to stand alone was to be swept away.

Still, not everyone welcomed her.

One lord spat at her feet, eyes cold with disdain. "Your blood may be royal, girl, but your path reeks of ruin."

Seren's blade had been half-drawn and his voice was a calm, unyielding promise, "She's the only reason the ruin hasn't already reached your front gate."

Nisrine said nothing. She simply turned and left. Those who wished to follow would. Those who didn't would soon understand why they should have.

Captain Aeron set out with Thalen, Axel, Lexa, Caelis, and his scouts, fanning through the hills to search for villages or hidden courts the old maps had overlooked. Meanwhile, Elaila and Dade vanished into the forest's deeper paths, intent on speaking with their clan leader.

As the nights grew colder and the sky turned stranger, her connection with Seren shifted too. There were no confessions, no grand declarations, only glances held a breath too long. The way his hand steadied her shoulder when disappointment pressed down on her after another failed meeting, how he never asked if she was all right. He simply knew.

And she found herself looking for him, listening for the soft footfall that told her he was near. When doubt crept in, it was his presence that steadied her. When she allowed herself to hope, he was the first face that came to mind.

They were no longer just childhood friends. Not anymore.

One night, camped at the border where Fae forest blurred into human hills, Nisrine stood alone, staring out at the strange horizon. Mist rolled across the ground in unnatural currents. Trees leaned toward her like they remembered her name. The sky was streaked with violet arcs of lightning that flickered and died.

Seren approached silently, his cloak dusted with frost. "The others are asleep," he said.

She nodded, not looking away from the horizon. "They won't be for long. The world's waking."

He stepped beside her, close enough that she could feel the warmth of him against the night. "And if it doesn't like what it sees?"

"Then we fight harder," she said.

He was quiet for a long moment. Then, softly, "You've changed."

"So have you."

A low breath escaped him, half a laugh, half something too soft to name. "I think we had to."

She turned to him. There was moonlight on his face, softening the shadows beneath his eyes. "I don't know what's coming, Seren. I don't know how to stop it."

"But you'll try."

She nodded once. "And I'll need you with me."

218

"I'm already with you, Nis," he said, simply. "I always have been."

No more words were needed.

Chapter 27

The forest grew colder as they descended toward the old catacombs.

What passed for a trail here was barely more than a stretch of withered roots and crumbling stone, leading down into a hollow nestled in the base of a cliff. The sun had not reached this place in centuries. Not even moonlight lingered long. It was as though the land itself bent around the domain of the vampires.

Nisrine paused at the threshold, the ground slick with lichen and stained with old blood. Magic pressed against her skin, dormant, yet expectant.

"He knows we're coming," Dade muttered, eyes scanning the tree line. "He always knows."

Beside her, Seren shifted, hand never far from the hilt of his sword. But his gaze remained on her.

"Are you sure about this?" he asked quietly. "Vampires don't make oaths lightly. And they don't fight for free."

"I don't expect them to," Nisrine replied. "But we can't win this without them. We need every ally willing to stand against Lonan."

She stepped forward, and the protection wards allowed her to pass.

A low vibration pulsed through the earth as the air thickened. One by one, the others followed: Seren, Dade, Elaila, Olesia, Mirell, and Corvan, until they emerged into a narrow cavern where fire flickered from sconces beautifully carved out of bone.

There, seated upon a throne of carved obsidian, was Lord Norrix.

He was as still as death; his form draped in dark robes that shimmered like oil. His eyes, black as ink with rings of silver, followed Nisrine's approach unblinkingly. Around him, the elders of the vampire clan stood like statues, their expressions unreadable, their silence more threatening than words.

Elaila, pale but whole, stepped forward from the shadows and nodded once to Nisrine. "I told him you'd come. How you saved me, and I owe you."

Lord Norrix rose.

The motion was slow, deliberate, yet full of restrained power. He descended the steps of his dais with the measured grace of a predator who knew he never needed to run.

"Nisrine of the Fallen Constalatia," he said, voice smooth as old wine. "Blood of Cherith. Daughter of War. Breaker of the gate. You come to me now, with the worlds bleeding into one. What is it you ask?"

She met his gaze, chin lifted, heart thudding.

"I ask for your alliance," she said. "The dark creatures are rising. King Lonan has made his pact with The Eidolon. If we don't unite, both realms will burn. You know this."

A ripple moved through the gathered vampires, an almost imperceptible shift. Not fear. Curiosity.

Lord Norrix studied her in silence.

"And what will you offer in return?"

Nisrine held his studying gaze. "A place in the world that comes after. One not ruled by Lonan's tyranny or bound by the old blood hierarchies. One where your kind don't have to serve as scapegoats for ancient fears and your clan won't have to hide in shadows."

Dade let out a low whistle. "Bold."

Lord Norrix's lips curved, not quite a smile.

"You speak of a world no one has yet survived to shape," he said. "But I see your heart. And I remember your mother's light."

He stepped closer, until they were only breaths apart. Seren tensed beside her.

"Will you swear it, Princess?" Lord Norrix asked, voice low. "On your blood and breath and name?"

Nisrine reached into her cloak and drew her dagger. She sliced a thin line across her palm and offered it.

"I swear it," she said. "By blood and breath and name."

Lord Norrix's fingers closed around hers, cold as stone. His own palm split, a drop of midnight falling into hers. A drop of bright red falling into his.

The oath bound them.

A tremor of magic crackled through the chamber. The sconces flared.

"Then the old pacts are broken," Lord Norrix said, voice echoing as if the walls themselves bore witness. "We will stand with you, Nisrine of the New World. My fangs are yours, and with them the dark will turn on its own."

He stepped back, and the elders bowed their heads.

Olesia exhaled at her side, quietly. "You did it."

Nisrine didn't answer. Her eyes remained on Lord Norrix's.

Because beneath the oath, beneath the momentary hope, she had seen something else in the vampire's expression. Something ancient and calculating.

They had gained an ally. But they had also awakened an old power.

The others remained behind, speaking in low tones with the vampire elders, but Nisrine slipped out into the upper corridor where the air wasn't so heavy with ash and ancient power.

Julie Nelson

The tunnel was narrow, lined with jagged rock and threads of moss that glowed faintly in the dark. It smelled of damp stone and something older, like dust from a sealed tomb, now cracked open. She exhaled slowly, pressing her palm against the cool wall. The sting from the blood oath still tingled, sharp and real.

Footsteps echoed behind her. She didn't need to turn.

"You always walk ahead of us when your thoughts are louder than your voice," Seren said, stopping a pace behind her.

She let out a quiet laugh, tired and hollow. "I didn't mean to."

"I know." A pause. "You did well in there."

She turned, leaning her back against the stone. His silhouette was lit only by the faint bioluminescence around them, his face half in shadow. But his eyes, always steady, always watching, were locked on hers.

"It didn't feel like winning," she said. "It felt like... inviting one storm to fight another."

"That's because it is."

"Helpful," she murmured.

He took a step closer. "But it was the right storm to choose."

She looked up at him, heart tight in her chest. "How can you be so sure?"

"I'm not," he admitted. "I'm never sure. But I've seen what Lonan is willing to do. I'd rather stand beside you in the eye of the storm than watch it swallow you from afar."

Silence pulsed between them, warm and full. She hadn't realized how close he'd gotten until she felt the heat of him, real and grounding.

She searched his face. "You've always followed me, Seren. Even when I didn't know where I was going."

"I don't follow you," he said, quiet and firm. "I choose to walk with you. There's a difference."

That struck something deep. Her throat tightened.

"You keep saying things like that," she whispered, "and I'm going to forget how to breathe."

He smiled, just barely. "You already have."

The words lingered in the charged space between them.

Then, without hesitation this time, Seren lifted his hand and touched her face, fingers brushing the curves of her lips like she was something precious. His touch was warm, steady, and hesitant only in the way that someone approaches something sacred.

Nisrine didn't move, didn't breathe. She just looked up into his eyes, and for a long heartbeat, neither of them said anything.

Then she leaned in, just enough.

And he met her there.

The kiss was soft. No urgency, no firestorm of passion. Just a quiet, reverent meeting of mouths that spoke more than either of them had been able to say out loud. A vow in the silence. A promise made without blood.

Her hands found the front of his cloak, curling in the fabric as she deepened the kiss just slightly. He let his forehead rest against hers when they finally pulled apart.

"I should have done that a long time ago," he said quietly.

"I wouldn't have been ready," she whispered back. "But now... I think I need it. I think I need *you*."

His thumb brushed her cheek again, and his voice was a murmur. "Then I'm yours."

She closed her eyes, letting the truth of that settle in her chest where it rooted, warm and sure, like the first light after a long night.

The storm was still coming. The war was still ahead. But for now, just for this breath, she was not a weapon, not a leader, not a princess.

She was just Nisrine in love with just Seren.

A lone, loose pebble clattered down the stone tunnel. Its small sound echoed as it bounced toward Nisrine's foot.

Seren tensed. Nisrine turned her head just enough to see who stood at the edge of the firelight. Flames danced across Corvan's face.

He didn't say anything at first. His expression was unreadable, blank, almost, but something in his stance betrayed the tension held beneath his stillness. His lips pressed into a thin line. His gaze flicked from Seren's hands on Nisrine's back to the tilt of her head against his chest, and then finally to her eyes.

She stepped away instinctively, suddenly aware of how it must look. But Seren didn't move.

Corvan raised one brow, cool, sharp, distant. "We were looking for you," he said. His voice was calm. Too calm. "Camp is set."

Nisrine nodded, brushing a stray curl behind her ear. "We just needed a moment."

Corvan didn't reply. He turned and walked away, his cloak billowing behind him, his shoulders held too tight, with something he didn't seem to understand himself.

Seren let out a quiet breath. "He knows."

"I know," Nisrine said softly. "But I don't know why he looked... hurt."

"He's not the type to admit it's hurt," Seren muttered, watching Corvan's retreating form. "That's the problem."

They followed in silence, returning to the rest of the group in their new camp where soft voices murmured between companions. But Corvan kept his distance.

He sat at the edge of the clearing, away from the firelight, eyes turned toward the trees but not seeing them. When Nisrine approached later with a quiet word on her lips, he stood and walked away without looking at her.

She watched him go, a knot forming in her throat.

"You're not responsible for his feelings," Seren said gently, appearing at her side.

"I know," she said. "But I still care."

Seren nodded. "So do I. But he'll either find peace with it... or he won't."

She didn't answer. She wasn't sure what peace looked like anymore.

Corvan moved through the trees like a shadow, far enough from the firelight that even the sounds of the camp faded to a dull hum. He stopped only when the air was still and cold enough to sting his lungs.

He sat on a moss-covered boulder and pressed his palms into his knees, grounding himself.

It shouldn't matter.

He had told himself that more times than he could count. Nisrine was not his. She never had been. She was powerful, luminous, made of something otherworldly, and he'd known from the start that whatever drew him to her was a thread not meant to be tugged.

But the image still burned behind his eyes. Her face tilted up toward Seren's. The quiet softness between them. The way she had leaned into his touch like it was home.

And it should not have mattered. But gods, it did.

He drew a slow, tense breath and looked skyward, through the skeletal canopy of trees, where the stars shimmered in a way they hadn't before the gate had broken. Even the heavens were changing. The world felt like it was unraveling thread by thread, and he couldn't find his footing in it.

It wasn't the kiss that undid him. It was what it meant. That she had chosen.

And maybe that was why it hurt.

Not because he'd loved her. He didn't, he told himself, not like that. But because for the first time since he'd clawed his way through life half-human and half-Fae, he'd felt a flicker of belonging near her. A sense that he wasn't just tolerated but seen. Known.

And now, he wasn't sure what was left of that.

He scrubbed a hand up his face, dragging his fingers through his hair. The jealousy tasted strange, sour, and unfamiliar. He wasn't used to wanting what he couldn't justify. He wasn't used to wanting anything at all.

A branch cracked behind him. Not close. Just a deer, maybe. Or Captain Aeron coming back from his scouting adventure.

Corvan stood slowly, shoving the feeling deep, where it couldn't claw at him.

He didn't have time to unravel. They were on the edge of war. And Nisrine... she was more than his feelings, more than a moment in the dark for someone who had already risked everything for her.

She was the storm at the heart of it all.

And he would still follow her.

Even if it burned.

Chapter 28

Smoke curled up into the dusky sky, black against twilight gold, rising in ragged spirals beyond the tree line. The scent reached them seconds later: scorched wood, burning fields… and something fouler. Something wrong.

It coated the back of Nisrine's throat like ash and tasted of iron, and for a moment, she couldn't breathe.

She stood slowly, her cloak rustling against the dry grass, eyes narrowing as the wind shifted again. Around her, the makeshift camp fell into a strange hush. Vampires, Fae, and humans paused mid-task, sharpening blades, mixing potions, whispering over maps. Heads turned toward the horizon. Someone cursed softly.

Then, "Make way!"

Captain Aeron staggered into the campfire's glow, armor scorched and cracked at the seams, his chest rising and falling in ragged heaves. His face was streaked with soot and blood, too much blood, and his left gauntlet was missing entirely.

"They've hit the human town of Bellwater." His voice cracked with urgency, the sound of a male who had run too far and seen too much. "No warning. Eidolon, gods, there were too many, they tore through the fields and the..."

Gasps broke out before he finished.

Maps were dropped. A scout bolted upright, knocking over a water basin. Steel sprang from scabbards like an echo of panic. Even the vampires tensed, their eyes glinting under the flickering firelight.

Olesia was the first to speak. She stepped forward, face full of fury, the wind catching the edge of her long black coat. "Casualties?"

Aeron wiped at his brow, smearing soot into his hairline. "Too many to count," he said hoarsely. "It wasn't a raid. It was a slaughter. They came from the east. Like they crawled out of the damn river."

A heavy silence fell.

Lord Norrix stood motionless as a carved statue, his shadow flickering long across the grass. The flames reflected in his dark eyes, though his face betrayed no emotion, only the subtle tightening of his jaw.

He leaned more heavily on his cane, the ivory grip carved like a serpent's skull, and exhaled through his nose. "So it begins."

His voice was soft. Not surprised. Not shaken.

231

Merely resigned.

Corvan stood beside Nisrine now, fist hovering over the hilt of his blade, knuckles white. "Bellwater is a farming village," he said. "Children. Farmers. They had no way to fight back."

"They didn't even get the chance," Aeron muttered. "The Eidolon moved like smoke, like they weren't bound to flesh. Arrows passed straight through some of them."

"They're testing us," Corvan said coldly. "Testing *her*."

All eyes turned to Nisrine.

She stood firm.

The fire cracked beside her, spitting sparks into the dark.

Her pulse pounded like war drums in her ears.

The command tent filled quickly. Maps were swept aside. Arguments flared like sparks.

"We should pull back to Norrix's stronghold," barked one of the human commanders, slamming a gauntleted fist on the table. "Fortify. Regroup. Let the Eidolon come to us next time."

"And let more die in the meantime?" snapped Olesia, her braid frayed and her eyes wild. "What happens when Bellwater is just the first? When it's the borderlands, the trading routes..." Her hands swept in frantic arcs over the map, "... everywhere?"

"We are not prepared for a full assault," snapped one of Lord Norrix's advisors, his voice as dry and sharp as old parchment. "If we spread too thin…"

"We've already lost ground," someone else barked. "Strike now, while they're still close, still exposed!"

The circle erupted. Allies now turned on one another with raised voices, heated gestures, wild-eyed panic wearing the mask of strategy. The very air inside the command tent felt tight, too full, too loud.

"We can't chase shadows without a plan," Corvan said sharply. His voice rose above the others, clipped and cold. "That's exactly what Lonan wants. Chaos. A fractured front."

"Tell that to the people already dead," Seren growled from across the room. His hands rested firmly on the table, his shoulders squared. "Tell it to the children pulled from the rubble."

A hush threatened, but only for a breath.

"Enough." Nisrine's voice cut through the room like a blade. Not loud, but sharp enough to silence them all.

The tent held its breath.

Her eyes, glowing faintly with the trace of lingering magic, swept the room. "We move," she said. Two words. Absolute.

Lord Norrix tilted his head with quiet approval, his mouth unreadable behind the long shadows cast by the fire.

Elaila's lips curved into something more dangerous than a smile. "Quick and lethal," she murmured. "I like it."

Corvan shifted beside the war table, his arms crossed. His frown deepened. "And when Lonan springs a trap?" he asked, low and tense.

Nisrine met his gaze evenly. "Then we'll break it."

A heartbeat passed. And then another.

Seren was already moving. "You lead," he said, his voice steady, sure. "We follow."

There was no hesitation in his eyes, only fire.

Nisrine nodded once. Her decision had been made long before the arguing began. The Eidolon wouldn't stop. Lonan wouldn't wait. And the more they hesitated, the more ground they would lose. Not just in territory, but in hearts, in trust, in the fragile hope that had bound these disparate forces together.

She turned toward the tent's entrance, her cloak catching the wind. "Ready the horses," she said. "Arm the camp. We ride before the next smoke touches the sky."

Behind her, the war council scattered like leaves caught in a storm.

The tent was empty now. The voices had gone, leaving only the fading echo of arguments and the low rustle of wind against canvas. Outside, preparations churned, steel clinking, horses snorting, shouted orders in the dusk. But within, all was still.

Nisrine stood near the war table, one hand braced on its edge. The maps had been swept into disarray, their lines smeared. The scent of ash clung to everything.

She exhaled slowly, a tremor barely hidden in her breath.

Behind her, boots scuffed quietly across the ground. She didn't turn, but she knew who it was by the way the silence shifted around him. How the air always felt warmer when he was near.

Seren's voice was soft. "You held them together."

"Barely." Her laugh was tired, breathless. "They listened because they were afraid. Not because they believed."

"I did," he said. "I always have."

She turned then. He stood close, closer than he usually allowed himself to be when others might see. Their eyes met. Something fragile passed between them.

"I'm scared," she admitted. "Not of the fight. Not of him. But of losing... the pieces of me that still feel like mine."

"You won't," he said. "I'll fight for those pieces if I have to."

Her breath caught at that. And then she closed the space between them.

His hand rose, brushing against her cheek, reverent in its slowness. "You don't have to be strong for everyone. Not right now."

"But I do," she whispered, even as she leaned into the touch. "That's the price."

He cupped her face fully then, his calloused thumb brushing beneath her eye as if he could wipe away more than exhaustion. "Then let me be your strength, not just for this moment. But for every moment you need it."

She didn't answer with words. Instead, she kissed him.

It was sudden, but not rushed. Fierce, but not careless. He pulled her close with an arm around her waist, the other still cradling her cheek.

The world outside could burn. For now, there was only this.

They parted slowly, foreheads pressed together, breaths mingling.

Outside, the horns began to sound, riders assembling, battle drawing near.

Chapter 29

The sky burned orange on the horizon, but it was nothing compared to the blaze on the ground.

Flames licked the rooftops like greedy tongues. Whole houses were swallowed by fire. Bellwater's once-golden wheat fields had been flattened and torn as if something massive had plowed through them. Smoke billowed high into the air, mixing with ash and the sharp sting of burning magic.

Then they saw them. Creatures like living nightmares prowled the outskirts of the village, hulking things made of shadow and bone, their forms flickering as if half-born from smoke. Limbs too long, jaws unhinged, bodies twisted by magic that had no right to exist in this world. The scent of rot and void curled through the air, thick as oil. The Eidolon.

The ground trembled beneath Nisrine's boots. Her fingers tightened around the hilt of her sword. Her heart raced as the storm of ancient magic roared through her, but she fought to keep her focus, to hold the line between the two forces. The Eidolon were closing in, rising like a tide that threatened to drown them all, but the strength of her own power, the magic of both the Fae and the darker forces within her, gave her the strength to push back.

A scream pierced the night.

Nisrine's head snapped toward the sound. A child bolted across a yard, clutching a younger sibling. Behind them, a beast unfurled itself from the shadows, teeth gleaming, claws raised.

A farmer burst from a barn, bloodied and barefoot, a creature snapping at his heels.

There were no defenses here. No warning. Just people. Ordinary people.

Nisrine inhaled deeply, forcing herself to find that delicate balance. She reached deep into herself, into the very core of her being, where both the light and the darkness lived in equal measures.

With a sharp exhale, she released her magic in a focused burst, a massive wave of energy that shot outward, pushing back the shadows like a tidal wave. The creatures screamed in pain as the light blasted them back, faltering for a moment. But Nisrine could feel the strain. It wasn't enough.

The others moved behind her.

The first Eidolon lunged. Her blade sang through the air, colliding with its malformed skull. A spray of black splattered across her armor, and the thing screamed, a sound too high, too wrong. Her magic surged with the blow, flowing into the strike and exploding from the wound like a burst of sunlight through fog.

To her right, Elaila became motion incarnate. Her body twisted mid-leap, her blade flashing with every twist, her fangs bared. She tore through an Eidolon with merciless precision, her eyes glowing red-gold in the firelight.

Lord Norrix advanced slowly, his cane discarded. Shadow poured from his fingertips like liquid smoke, wrapping around an Eidolon's limbs and tearing them apart with surgical grace. He murmured in the ancient tongue, his magic elegant, brutal.

And Dade... Dade laughed like the fight had been promised to him in a dream. He whirled between enemies, dual blades flashing. "Bet all you ugly bastards bleed the same!" he shouted gleefully, pinning two Eidolon to the ground with a dancer's flourish. "Oh. Nope. That's new. Gross!"

Corvan's voice cut through the cacophony, calm and commanding. "They're weaker in the legs! Aim low! They vanish in fire but regroup in shadow. Light the fields! Force them into the open!"

Flames bloomed as his orders took shape.

Nisrine moved as if the battle was part of her breath. Her sword met claws, fangs, and bones. Her magic lashed out in controlled arcs, wind to scatter, flame to burn, light to blind. Every strike, every spell was instinct and choice combined. Seren fought at her side, not behind, not ahead, like rhythm beside melody, different but moving as one, blades spinning, catching enemies mid-leap and slamming them into the dirt.

"On your left," he called, and her shield arm swung up without hesitation.

The impact nearly knocked her off her feet, but he was there, steady, unshakable.

"You good?" he asked between blows.

She grinned; blood streaked across her cheek. "Absolutely."

They pressed forward.

Olesia cleared a burning stable and dragged a pair of wounded villagers behind her. Lord Norrix redirected a swarm of flickering creatures into a collapsed well, sealing them with a single gesture. Dade leapt from the remains of a fence, landing on an Eidolon's back with a whoop. "Should've stayed in the nightmare realm, bitch!"

But still, they came.

The air was thick with smoke and shrieks, both human and not. Ash rained down like snow. The line between earth and sky blurred in the haze of firelight.

Nisrine saw a cluster of survivors huddled near the chapel, surrounded by half-formed beasts that clicked and slithered over stones.

A cry burst from her lips, not of fear, but of war song, and her magic ignited in full. Light and dark braided around her, a glowing inferno that surged as she raised her sword and carved a path through the dark.

"GO!" she shouted to the villagers. "RUN!"

The humans scattered and the Eidolon threatened to follow, but Seren and Thalen were there, slashing them down in a whirlwind of silver. Elaila and Corvan flanked the last one, twin blurs of wrath and calculation.

It felt endless. The burning. The screaming. The fight for every inch.

But slowly, inch by bloody inch, they began to push the monsters back.

The Eidolon faltered. Their snarls lost force. Their shapes flickered like candlelight struggling in the wind.

Then, the last of them scattered into ash and vanished.

Nisrine stood in the silence that followed, chest heaving, sword dripping with black. Her hair clung to her face.

Around her, the others regrouped, bloodied, winded, but alive.

Flames crackled where they still clung to ruined rooftops. A child sobbed somewhere behind a ruined wall. A young woman sat stunned beside a broken well, blood trailing from her scalp. A man called out for his wife. Horses cried out somewhere unseen. The village was broken but not completely lost.

But even as she looked around at the bodies, human and creature both, Nisrine felt it in her bones. This hadn't been the war. This had only been a warning.

Corvan stepped beside her, the wind tugging at his hair in complete disarray. "This was a probe," he said grimly. "Lonan's watching."

Nisrine didn't look at him. "He knows where I am now."

"He always did," Olesia murmured from where she knelt beside a wounded villager, her hands sticky with blood.

"But now," Nisrine said, her voice hoarse, "he knows I'm ready."

No one spoke. Not Seren, standing just behind her, his blades still dripping. Not Dade, who sat cross-legged on a

241

broken cart, face unusually solemn. Not Lord Norrix, whose silhouette loomed in the smoke like a statue of old.

But they all knew.

Bellwater wasn't just a village. It was a message.

Lonan had spoken. Nisrine had answered.

Chapter 30

The group moved through the wreckage, boots crunching over blackened wheat and splintered beams. Smoke clung to them like a second skin. Every face was streaked with sweat and soot. Some bore cuts across cheeks, down forearms, bleeding slowly, unnoticed. No one complained. They were searching. For survivors. For signs of life beneath ruin.

The smoke eventually cleared, but the silence left in its place pressed down on them like a shroud.

They buried the fallen at dawn.

The fields outside Bellwater, once golden with wheat, were now churned to gray. A patch of earth beneath a half-burned tree offered the only softness left. Nisrine knelt beside the nearest grave as the last clods of dirt fell, her hands stained with more than just blood.

Seren had seen battle before. Skirmishes at the edges of Constalatia, political feints dressed in steel. But this was different. This has been farmers, children, and elders. None of them stood a chance.

No one spoke.

Elaila stood with arms crossed, face unreadable. Dade's usual smirk had vanished and he stared far beyond the graves. Lord Norrix held a single black lily, an offering from the night, and placed it gently at the foot of the half-burned tree.

Corvan stood at the edge of the circle, apart from them, arms folded. He said nothing, but he stayed.

Olesia stepped up beside Nisrine, the wind tugged at her loose braid. "This wasn't your doing," she said quietly.

Nisrine's voice was low, raw. "Lonan's creatures came because of me."

Olesia didn't argue. She only rested a hand on Nisrine's shoulder. "Then make sure they never do again."

They stood together as the sun broke the horizon, red light spilling across the scorched land.

When the others turned to leave, Nisrine lingered. Her hand brushed the hilt of her blade, the leather cool against her skin. Not for defence. For a promise.

"You're not forgotten," she said quietly to the rows of fresh earth. She straightened, and when she spoke again, her voice carried like a vow. "We will burn him to the ground."

The wind carried ash through the fields, but beneath it, there was something else. A whisper of resolve threading through the morning.

She turned and followed the others.

War was coming.

And this time, it had a name.

The war table was nothing more than a scorched plank balanced precariously between two cracked crates, but it bore a gravity as heavy and immovable as stone. Around it stood faces marked by exhaustion and determination. Nisrine took her place at the head, her eyes sharper now, clearer, edged with a hard resolve.

Maps lay sprawled across the worn surface, corners pinned with daggers. Burn marks scarred their edges, ink smeared from sweat and ash. Elaila moved with a predator's grace, circling the table slowly, her gaze piercing as she studied the terrain markers. Dade leaned on a broken beam, arms crossed, expression unusually grim. His eyes, sharp and calculating, flicked between the maps and the faces gathered there.

Lord Norrix's fingers danced through the air above the maps, weaving subtle illusions that shimmered and flickered: glowing sigils marking key strongholds, shadowed trails tracing hidden enemy movements, and the fragile web of control Lonan had spun across the eastern spine of the forest.

"We can't strike Lonan directly," Corvan said, voice firm. "Not yet. But we can hurt him. Cut supply lines, unravel his command structure."

"Elaila and I can move faster without the rest of the forces," Dade added. "Hit smaller targets. Spread fear like he did here."

"No." Nisrine's voice was clear, her mouth set in a tight, unyielding line. "We don't become what he is. Our strikes must be deliberate. Purposeful. Not cruel."

Elaila arched a skeptical eyebrow. "Then give us something worthy of precision."

Seren stepped forward, voice low but confident, "We take Blackfen. It's become one of Lonan's key outposts. Lightly guarded from the last scout reports. It's a waypoint between his camps and the larger command post near the fractured gate."

Corvan's gaze sharpened. "If we take Blackfen, we sever a crucial channel of his control."

Elaila smiled, teeth sharp. "That's worthy."

Nisrine planted her hand on the map. "Blackfen, then. We draw him out. Make him bleed resources. But we do more than strike. We send a message. We need to put a sigil on the gates. One Lonan will be sure to see."

"I can make it burn," Axel said. "Just enough to catch the sky."

"And I can make it whisper," Lexa murmured. "To remind him whose blood now stains his hands."

The twin spellcasters grinned broadly.

Nisrine nodded. "We don't wait for him to choose the battlefield again. We take the fight to him."

Seren leaned in, tapping a route with his finger. "We split into two groups. Fast and lethal, Dade, Elaila, Thalen, Riven, and me. You," he looked to Nisrine, "lead the forward push. A show of strength."

"She shouldn't be on the front lines," Corvan shook his head, concern darkening his features. "Not yet."

"She *has* to be," Seren countered. "They need to see her. The world needs to see her."

"I'm going," Nisrine said, leaving no room for debate. "We hit Blackfen before the week turns."

A silence followed. Not disagreement, but acceptance.

Olesia, who had stood quietly behind Nisrine's chair, stepped closer. She spoke softly, but every ear heard her. "She won't go alone. Not while I breathe. When you stand at the front, I'll be there behind you. And make sure Lonan knows this was the moment everything turned."

A murmur of approval rippled around the table. Quiet but certain.

The wind howled. But within the group, something stronger stirred. Resolve. Purpose. The shape of vengeance not just taken, but earned.

Chapter 31

As the meeting broke, the murmurs of preparation stirred. She glanced around at her allies. Each carried their own burdens, their own scars.

Axel and Lexa left immediately to send their message.

Nisrine took a deep breath, tasting embers and dust, and felt the pulse of magic beneath the soil, restless and eager. A reminder that the world was shifting beneath their feet.

Seren was already moving to rally the scouts. Elaila slipped away with the grace of a shadow, and Dade leaned in close to Corvan, speaking in urgent, clipped tones.

Nisrine was left alone for a moment. She looked at the maps once more, tracing the lines toward Blackfen with trembling fingers. The place was more than a waypoint. It was a symbol of Lonan's hold on the land, a choke point that, if lost, could unravel his grip entirely.

A quiet shift of movement drew her gaze. Olesia, gathering scattered parchments from the edge of the table. Their eyes met briefly. No words passed between them, but there was a steadiness there, a silent promise that Nisrine would not face this alone.

The fury that had risen in her moments ago settled into a burning resolve. This was strategic, but it was also for every life Lonan had crushed, every village left in ruin. And for those still standing, holding the line beside her.

She rose, steadying herself. Lonan was waiting.

And Nisrine would meet him head-on.

The great hall of Blackfen's fortress echoed with the clamor of victory. Torches flared against the stone walls, casting jagged shadows over faces flushed with triumph. King Lonan stood tall on the dais, his dark cloak billowing behind him like a storm cloud come to life. Around him, generals and captains drank deeply, laughter ringing sharp and hollow.

He let them revel, for now. The taste of victory was bitter and sweet all at once, but it was his to savor. The human settlement was shattered.

Lonan's eyes scanned the room, piercing and cold, stopping briefly on the faces of those who had served him well. Their loyalty was tested in fire, and none had faltered. Not since Nisrine slipped through the gate before shattering it had his fury found a proper outlet. Tonight was a declaration: his reach was still long, his wrath unbroken.

A grizzled captain stepped forward, bearing a tattered banner stolen from the villagers, its colors were singed but still vivid. "My king, Bellwater has fallen. The Eidolon did their job."

Lonan's lips curled into a thin smile. "Good. Let none forget what happens to those who stand against my crown."

The hall erupted into cheers. Lonan raised his hand, silencing the noise with ease. "But this is only the beginning. Our enemy thinks to hide behind forests and in the shadows. They underestimate us."

He moved toward the long, rough-hewn table at the center of the hall. Spread across it were maps, carved with intricate marks and notes in spidery script. The product of relentless scouting and dark divination. A hand pressed on the map's surface, fingers splayed over the region that Nisrine now called home.

A shadow flickered at the edge of the room, and Lonan's gaze sharpened. His advisor, a tall figure cloaked in black robes, stepped forward with a slow bow.

"My king," the advisor intoned, "our scouts have reported increased activity near the front gate. Strange markings... a sigil, burning with magic."

Lonan's eyes narrowed. "Show me."

The advisor raised his hand, and in the flicker of torchlight, an illusion blossomed above the map. A glowing sigil, its lines shifting like smoke caught on a wind. It burned faintly red and gold, whispering in a language older than the stones beneath their feet.

Lonan's fingers clenched into a fist at his side, his eyes flicking sharply to the flowing sigil. It was a message. A challenge. And it carried the unmistakable mark of Nisrine.

"They mock me?" he asked, voice clearly shocked. "They think their petty symbols can turn the tide?"

The hall grew still. Even the torches seemed to gutter in hesitation.

"But they forget," Lonan said, stepping closer to the map. "This war is not theirs to win. I will crush them body and soul. And when I am finished, no trace of rebellion will remain."

Outside, the wind howled through the broken windows, carrying the faint, eerie whispers of the sigil's magic. Lonan's smile was thin but certain. The game had changed. And he would not be caught unprepared.

Lonan dismissed the gathered guards with a flick of his hand. One by one, they filtered out of the hall, their footsteps echoing in the cold silence. Only the advisor lingered, the shadow of the sigil still hanging between them.

When the door finally closed, Lonan turned to the embers crackling in the hearth. For a moment, the scent of burning wood drew him back, far from this ruined hall and the whispered voices of ghosts.

Long ago, before he became the king, he had been a boy beneath the shadow of an ancient throne.

The halls of his father's keep had always been cold. Stone corridors dark, damp, and unwelcoming, haunted by the echoes of old magic. He had learned early that warmth was a luxury, and affection even more so. His father's lessons had been carved in iron and flame. Each one a brutal reminder of what endured. These were the only truths he had even known.

"Power is not given," the old king had told him, voice gravel-deep, "it is *taken*. And you take it with *fear*."

Lonan remembered the flicker of the hearth that night, the glow of embers that danced like spirits in the darkness. His father had set a small birdcage on the table, a tiny wren caught in a snare.

"You see, boy," he said, fingers drumming against the iron bars. "This creature is small. Fragile. It sings even when it knows the sky is gone. But it will die here. Because it is *weak*. It will fly out, driven by hope it doesn't have." He cracked the cage open with a snap. The bird fluttered free for a moment, a brief, beautiful arc of motion.

Then his father's hand closed around it, crushing it without hesitation.

Lonan had felt something cold and resolute settle in his bones that night. He understood, then, what the world required: the willingness to break the song of another to keep fear in the hearts of all. To have power over all.

Now, standing in Blackfen's hall, he traced that lesson across the decades. It was etched into his very skin, the iron law that had shaped him.

The flickering sigil's whispers brought him back. He studied its shifting lines, not just a challenge, but a reminder of every lesson he had been taught.

He would not be the bird in the cage. He would not let anyone else's song drown out his rule.

Lonan let the memory fade, letting the cold settle back around his heart. He turned to the advisor. "Let the captains rest, but the hunters, I want them moving before dawn."

The advisor bowed. "As you command, my king."

Lonan watched him go, then turned back to the illusion of the sigil. He let his fingers hover over its phantom heat, feeling the distant pull of the magic that had birthed it. Nisrine's mark. Her defiance. Her promise.

A faint smile curved his lips, not of joy, but of certainty.

"Let her think she has found her strength," he murmured to the embers. "Let her gather her warriors and forge her vows."

His eyes narrowed. The fire cracked in answer.

"I will break them all."

Chapter 32

Bright eyes glinted in the thin light of dawn. The twin spellcasters were perched like sentinels atop the jagged outcrop overlooking the valley below.

"It's done," Lexa declared, her voice light with satisfaction. "The binding is set. Lonan's force will have to work twice as hard to pull energy from the leyline now."

Axel chuckled. "Twice as hard? More like threefold. Even the old fox will feel the sting of that."

They made their way back to the camp that the others had set up at the edge of Bellwater. Walking taller and smiling broader, the twins' pride was contagious. It carried a spark of defiance that warmed the forest's gloom. Nisrine watched them with a quiet smile at their triumph, her breath turning to mist in the cold morning air.

"Well done you two," she said softly. "Let him know we're no longer running."

Seren stood beside her, his dark hair tangled from the wind, eyes focused with a soldier's practicality. But when he turned to her, his expression softened.

"You gave them the idea," he said, a faint smile touching his lips. "You're the reason we're here."

Nisrine's gaze met his, and for a moment, the looming threat of battle seemed to fade. In that sliver of time, there was only the hush of the forest, the flicker of trust between them, an unspoken promise neither had dared to name.

"We're all the reason," she murmured. "Every one of us."

Corvan shifted his weight behind them, his face half-hidden beneath the hood of his traveling cloak. His eyes, though, betrayed him, brimming with a storm he'd never voiced. Nisrine could see it in the way his jaw tightened, the restless twitch of his fingers at his side.

"We've taken a risk," he said quietly, his tone measured, though his voice roughened at the edges. "Lonan's no fool. If he senses the sigil's interference, he'll strike back. Hard."

Seren's brow furrowed. "That's why we're here. We're ready."

"Ready?" Corvan's gaze cut to him, then back to Nisrine. "When he feels his hold slipping. You're not..." He broke off, exhaling a ragged breath. "We have to be sure we're not just inviting ruin."

Nisrine stepped closer, her fingers brushing against Corvan's sleeve. "Corvan," she said softly, "I know the danger. I know what he is. But I'm not turning back."

For a heartbeat, his eyes met hers, and she saw the weight he carried. The burden of ancient memory, the ache of truths he'd carried alone for too long. Then he looked away, shoulders tense.

Off to the side, Olesia's gaze lingered on Corvan longer than most would notice. She wasn't smiling, but there was a quiet curiosity in her eyes, as if she were trying to read the shadows in his expression.

When Nisrine's glance slid toward her, Olesia only lifted a brow, saying nothing.

"Just… be certain," he said hoarsely. "You're not just fighting him. You're fighting everything he's twisted."

A hush fell over them, and the twins stilled, their chatter gone. Nisrine felt the tremor of what they were about to face. So close now she could almost taste the iron tang of it on the wind.

But instead of fear, she felt only clarity.

"I am certain," she said firmly. "We're not pieces on his board. We're more than that. And together, we'll break whatever hold he still thinks he has."

Dade let out a low whistle. "Well said, Princess," he murmured, his grin returning. "Can't argue with that."

Elaila stepped forward, her hand resting on the hilt of her slender blade. "Then let's finish the preparations," she said. "The sigil is set, but we'll need to anchor it with the moon ritual tonight. I'll start gathering the ash."

"Take Axel and Lexa with you," Seren said, his tone cool but steady. "We'll need the right materials, and they know what to look for."

Elaila gave a brisk nod, already moving.

Riven stretched, rolling his shoulders as he scanned the forest. "I'll go with them," he said lightly. "Keep everyone out of trouble."

Lira took a bite of an apple and stated, "I'm coming too."

As they disappeared into the trees, Nisrine turned her focus to the others. The clearing had become a makeshift camp: a small fire crackled at the center, sending sparks into the pale sky. Dade stood apart from the flame, his sharp gaze following Elaila's departure.

"They'll be careful," Nisrine said. "But we need to be ready if Lonan's hunters catch wind of us. We've only bought ourselves time."

Seren nodded. "We'll set up perimeter wards. I want them woven tight, no gaps."

Caelis, who'd been carefully copying sections of Queen Cherith's notes onto clean parchment, looked up. "I can help," he offered. "There are older warding patterns here. They're harder to break."

Seren gave him a nod of approval. "Good. Let's get them in place before sunset."

Olesia lingered near the fire, her gaze drifting repeatedly to where Corvan stood just beyond the circle, his hood shadowing his face. Her fingers absently traced the edge of her cloak as she watched him.

Nisrine's eyes flicked toward Olesia and then back to Corvan, a knowing smile tugging at her lips. She sat next to her with a huff and said "He's not easy to read, is he?"

Olesia shook her head slowly. "No. But there's something in his silence. Something he carries."

Nisrine's eyes softened. "Be careful not to shoulder more than you can bear."

Olesia met her gaze steadily. "I want to understand. If I can, maybe I can help."

As the group moved with purpose, Nisrine felt the hum of the broken gate still pulsing in her veins. A reminder of what they'd done, of the thin line they now walked between defiance and doom.

She patted Olesia's shoulder and walked toward the edge of the clearing, where the forest pressed close and the air was thick with the scent of moss. For a moment, she let herself close her eyes, feeling the quiet rush of power in the earth beneath her boots, the echo of magic in the air.

A soft rustle behind her drew her back. She turned to find Seren watching her, his expression unreadable.

"You're thinking too loudly again," he said gently, stepping closer.

She let out a soft laugh, though it trembled a little. "Am I?"

His hand brushed against hers, the faintest touch, but enough to send a warmth spiraling through her chest. "I know you," he said. "You carry everyone's hopes like they're your own. But you don't have to do it alone."

She met his gaze, her heart catching in her throat. "I'm not alone," she whispered. "I guess I never have been. Not really."

He smiled, small and fleeting, but real. His fingers curled around hers, grounding her in a way that went beyond magic, beyond duty.

But before she could say more, a quiet voice broke the moment.

"Seren," Corvan said from the shadows of the trees. "We need to talk."

The moment slipped away like water through her fingers. Seren gave her hand a final squeeze, then stepped back, his expression shifting back to the commander's calm focus.

"I'll be back," he murmured, and then he was gone, following Corvan deeper into the forest.

Nisrine watched them disappear, a flicker of unease threading through her chest. She knew the tension that still simmered between them. The clash of purpose and the tangle of feelings that no one dared to name.

She turned back to the clearing, her mind already racing ahead.

They spent the day in quiet labor, weaving wards and gathering what they could from the forest's edge. Elaila, Riven, and the twins returned with bundles of dried herbs. Caelis worked tirelessly, etching glyphs of protection into the stones that ringed their camp.

"It's done," Lira said, her breath clouding in the air. "The feather ash, the binding roots. Everything we need for tonight."

Seren nodded. "Good. We'll start as soon as the moon rises."

As night fell, they gathered in a circle around the fire. The flickering light painted their faces in gold and shadow, the air thick with the scent of burning sage. Nisrine knelt at the center, her hands were steady despite the tremor she felt in her bones. Caelis laid the parchment out, the ink shimmering faintly in the firelight.

"It has to be your blood," he said quietly. "It's the anchor. The final piece."

She nodded, her pulse a steady drum in her ears. She drew a small blade from her belt, the silver gleaming.

"I'm ready," she said.

A hush fell. Even the forest seemed to hold its breath.

She pressed the blade to her palm, the sting sharp and bright. Blood welled, red and vivid, and she let it drip onto the glyph.

A shiver ran through the air. The sigils flared, lines of ink and ash glowing softly as the magic took hold.

Seren watched her with a fierceness that was almost a prayer, his jaw went still as carved marble.

Corvan stood at the edge of the circle, his expression unreadable. But when their eyes met, she saw the storm in him. The way his fingers twitched like he wanted to reach out and pull her back, to shield her from the cost of this choice.

But he said nothing.

The ritual was a quiet thing. No grand gestures, no thunderous chants. Just breath and blood and the hum of the earth answering in kind. When it was done, the sigils pulsed once, then stilled, the magic settled into the bones of the land.

Nisrine exhaled, the ache in her hand already forgotten. Mirell and Olesia were already tending to the cut.

"It's done," she said softly.

Seren reached for her, his hand gentle on her shoulder. "You did it."

She leaned into his touch, her eyes closing briefly.

And when she looked up again, Corvan was gone.

Later, when the camp was quiet, she found him at the edge of the clearing. He stood alone, his cloak drawn tight around him, his gaze lost in the darkness beyond the trees.

"You're angry," she said quietly.

Corvan didn't turn. "I'm... worried," he admitted. "For you. For all of us."

She stepped closer. "We knew what we were walking into."

He let out a soft, mirthless laugh. "That's what frightens me the most. You're willing to risk everything... and I'm terrified I'll lose you before I can..."

His voice trailed off, but the words hung there, heavy as the winter air.

Before I can tell you.

Before I can let you go.

She reached out, her fingers brushing his arm. "Corvan," she said softly. "You don't have to hold back. Not here. Not with me."

For a moment, he was still. Then he turned to her, his eyes raw and searching. "I wish I could be the one you turned to," he said hoarsely. "I wish I could be enough."

Her breath caught in her throat. "You are... you're part of this. Part of us."

He gave a faint, sad smile. "But not the part of you that he holds."

Nisrine shook her head. "That doesn't make you less. You're my friend, my ally," she huffed a small laugh, "my berry buddy," she said with a gentle nudge. "I... I care about you, Corvan."

His shoulders sagged, and he let out a matching huffed laugh. "That will have to be enough."

She watched him a moment longer, then leaned forward, pressing her forehead to his. A quiet, wordless comfort.

They stood that way until the cold crept in, until the fire in the clearing began to fade.

Chapter 33

They emerged from their camp at dawn, the cold breath of winter biting at their cheeks. Nisrine walked at the front, her closest allies at her sides. They moved as one, every step a vow forged in the quiet dark of rebellion.

Blackfen rose before them, black stone spires clawing at the sky, a fortress steeped in dark magic. At the gates stood Lonan, flanked by his guards itching for payback, and the monstrous forms of the Eidolon.

The wind tugged at Lonan's cloak, and the ancient sigils on his armor glowed faintly with stolen magic.

For the first time in months, Nisrine met her father's gaze. His eyes were ice, his mouth twisting in something like a smile. He tilted his head, his voice a low rumble that dragged out both syllables, "Nisriiiiine...."

His tone was almost a caress, if not for the unmistakable venom in it. She stood her ground, the wind snapping at her cloak.

Lonan's gaze flicked past her to Seren, to Corvan, to Lord Norrix, to the allies who dared stand with her. "Such loyalty," he mused, cold amusement in his tone. "Such... foolishness."

But her resolve didn't falter. "This ends now. One way or another."

Lonan's knowing smile grew sharper. "We shall see."

Nisrine looked to Seren who met her gaze. His lips pressed tight and he gave her a nod. She took a step forward, raising her voice, "Father, it doesn't..."

Her words were cut off by Lonan raising his hand. His guards moved in unison. From the shadows, they pulled a cage. Tall, Fae-sized, covered with a dark cloth that fluttered in the biting air.

Nisrine's breath caught. She forced her feet to stay rooted, though every instinct screamed to run.

Lonan moved his hand up and down the cloth, then said with a voice as smooth as silk, "This is the cost of your rebellion. One life, for your defiance."

A low murmur rippled through the group. Eyes darted around, taking attendance to see who was missing. The world seemed to slow, to hold its breath. Nisrine's hands shook, grief and fury warring in her chest.

Lonan watched the group, his eyes gleaming with amusement.

On Fallen Wings

Finally, he nodded to his advisor.

The cloth was torn away, as gasps rang out through Nisrine's ranks.

Beneath the cloth stood a female draped in chains, her silver hair tangled and falling in waves down her hunched frame. Once regal and radiant, she now looked hollowed by captivity and torment. But when her head lifted, slowly, shakily, and her eyes found Nisrine's, the resemblance was undeniable.

Hazel met hazel.

"Mother," Nisrine breathed, the word as fragile as glass on her tongue.

Cherith blinked once.

Olesia's breath hitched, and a sudden, raw sob escaped her throat. Sharp and unexpected. She pressed a hand to her mouth.

And then, without warning, Lonan raised his hands. Darkness exploded outward in a cloud of thick, unnatural smoke, swallowing the space between them. Magic tore through the clearing in a rush of pressure and sound.

When it cleared, he was gone.

So were the guards and Eidolon.

So was the cage.

So was the queen.

Silence fell thick and choking.

Nisrine took trembling steps toward where her mother had just been and froze.

At her feet, something small and strange shimmered against the cold black rocks. A single leaf pulsed once with soft, living light. She knelt slowly, fingers brushing over its edge. She picked it up gently. The leaf pulsed again, then whispered, *"Find the door I left behind."*

Nisrine's breath caught. Behind her, the wind shifted. She turned to face the others. Her voice was quiet, but it rang like a blade drawn in the dark, "She's alive. And he's running."

Corvan stepped to her right. Seren to her left. Neither spoke. They didn't have to. They were with her.

As the wind carried the scent of magic and ruin, Nisrine's eyes narrowed as she said, "Let the coward run. The shadows he hides in will become his tomb."

On Fallen Crowns

Book Two Coming Soon.

She crossed realms for truth. Now she crosses blades for war.

Acknowledgments

I began this story as a sixteen-year-old kid who just wanted to be an author, scribbling down worlds that felt far bigger than I was. I never imagined the journey would eventually lead me here, holding the finished book in my hands. Along the way, I've been lucky enough to have people who believed in me even when my drafts were messy, my confidence shaky, and my coffee intake alarming.

To my family: Leslie, Shane, Carter, and Emma. Thank you for your endless encouragement and patience. You listened to me ramble about plot twists that didn't make sense yet, and characters who refused to behave. I couldn't have made it here without you.

To my friends: you know who you are. Thank you for cheering me on when I doubted myself, and for reminding me to step away from the keyboard once in a while and actually live life outside the page.

To my amazing editor, Olivia Rose: thank you for being both sharp-eyed and kind-hearted. Your quick replies and thoughtful notes kept me grounded, and your fun personal comments made me feel like I wasn't just sending chapters into the void but sharing them with a friend.

To my wonderful alpha readers: Serena, Leslie, Cait, Shane, and Robert. Thank you for giving your time, eyes, and hearts to this story. Your feedback helped me shape these pages

On Fallen Wings

into something stronger, sharper, and braver. You caught the cracks, filled in the gaps, and helped me see what was working even when I couldn't.

Finally, to every reader holding this book now: you're the reason stories survive. Thank you for stepping into this world with me. May you find pieces of yourself among the shadows and light, and may the story linger long after the last page turns.

And yes, I promise the sequel is already in the works.

About the Author

Julie Nelson writes about fae, vampires, and rebellions by night. When she isn't dreaming up new stories, she enjoys spending time with her children, a good book, and a strong cup of coffee. This is her debut novel, with many more worlds still to come.

TikTok: @julienelsonauthor
Instagram: @julienelsonauthor
julienelsonauthor.com
https://linktr.ee/julienelsonauthor